NIGHTMARES

VAMPIRE TWINS

A TRILOGY

THREE BOOKS IN ONE

Lions

NIGHTMARES

Vampire Twins 3

BLOODCHOICE

Janice Harrell

CHAPTER
ONE

ARI MONTCLAIR PUSHED OPEN THE FRENCH DOORS and stepped from the garden into the dining room. Her heart was pounding so hard, she felt sick. Voices were coming from the front of the house. Drawing closer to the living room, she slipped quietly down the hallway, then stood outside its door, listening.

"Her parents found the body at about two A.M.," said a gruff voice. "We're not accusing you of anything, son, but I think it would be better if your guardian were present. When do you expect your aunt to get home?"

The police have come for Paul! Ari thought, her heart contracting. She stepped into the living room. The impulse to help her twin overwhelmed her.

"Hullo," she said. The two police officers looked at her in surprise, and she suddenly felt dizzy. In their uniforms they looked solid and

1

imposing, monuments of authority. Their small, hard eyes bored into her.

"Ari, Susannah's dead!" Paul cried. "She's been murdered!"

He sounded so distressed that if Ari had not helped him move Susannah's body out of his car, she might have believed he was innocent. Carefully she avoided meeting his eyes.

"I know," she said, gulping hard. "Amanda told me about it when I was at the mall. I meant to tell you when you woke up."

"I've had the flu, Officer," Paul explained. "That's why I took Susannah home early last night. She and I went out for pizza, then I took her straight home." He shook his head. "It's hard to believe. I guess I can't take it in. It's like a bad dream." He glanced at Ari. "I was back here by eight o'clock, wasn't I, Ari?" His eyes pleaded with her not to betray him.

Ari nodded. "I fixed Paul some hot chicken soup," she said. "And he went straight to bed."

"You didn't go out again that night?" one of the officers asked him.

Paul shook his head. "I felt too rotten to roll over, much less to go out."

"I can swear to that," said Ari. "I have the room right next to Paul's. We had the connecting door between the rooms open in case he needed me. He didn't even get out of bed. What happened, Officer?"

"We aren't at liberty to say." The fat officer glanced at the other man.

2

"We should call Aunt Gabrielle at work, Paul," Ari said. "There must be some way they could get word to her. She teaches night classes, Officer."

"I think you had better do that," said the fat officer.

Ari went to the kitchen and scanned the message board, looking for Aunt Gabrielle's work number. Just then she heard the front door open, and Aunt Gabrielle's voice trilled, "I'm home, darlings!"

Ari leaned against the refrigerator and sighed with relief. She didn't have to go back to the living room. Aunt Gabrielle and Paul could handle the police.

The phone rang and Ari snatched it up.

"Hello?"

"Hello, Ari? Sybil." Ari scarcely recognized her friend's voice. "Have you told Paul about Susannah yet?" Sybil asked. "How's he taking the news?"

"I'm not sure. The police are here with him now," said Ari.

"Oh, no! How horrible. Are they acting like they suspect him?"

"I don't know. He explained that he took Susannah home early, but I don't know if they believed him."

"What a lucky thing you left my house when you did!" cried Sybil. "You can give him an alibi! Poor Paul! To have the police treating him like a criminal—what a nightmare!"

3

"Don't worry—I won't tell Paul what Amanda said. I've got to go now. The police must have left. Aunt Gabrielle wants to talk to me. Bye, Syb." Ari hung up and turned around to face her aunt.

"I'm so worried, Ari," Aunt Gabrielle said, wringing her fingers. Her large emerald ring glimmered against the whiteness of her hand. "Paul did it, didn't he?"

Ari nodded, unable to speak.

"We can't let the police put him in jail. One ray of sunlight could . . ." She let the thought go unfinished. "We must protect him at all costs," she finally choked out.

Paul came up behind his aunt and put his hands on her shoulders. The resemblance between them was eerie. They both had the same unearthly sort of beauty. The loose curls of Paul's black hair brushed his collar. He had strong black brows and well-defined cheekbones—and his face was as smooth and ghostly white as if it were made of plastic.

Of course they look alike, Ari thought. *They're both vampires.*

"Do you think the police believed me?" Paul asked.

"Why shouldn't they believe you?" said Ari. "I gave you an alibi."

"I'm not sure how much that will matter, Paul," said Aunt Gabrielle. "They might think your twin would lie for you."

Ari quickly turned away. *I've not only lied,*

she thought. *I've been his accomplice.*

"Goodness, Paul," cried Aunt Gabrielle, drawing away from him. "What's that you've got on your fingers?"

Paul held up his hands and regarded them ruefully. His fingertips were covered with an inky black substance. "They took my fingerprints."

Ari stared at him. "Do you *have* fingerprints?"

"Yup." He smiled. "Don't worry, Ari. Vampires have fingerprints."

"You didn't touch anything at Susannah's house, did you?" asked Aunt Gabrielle.

"No. We wore gloves," said Paul. "Ari's idea."

"That's something, anyway," said Aunt Gabrielle grudgingly. "What can have possessed you to kill Susannah, Paul? Someone you know! Your girlfriend! Naturally the police would suspect you in such a case."

"It was an accident," protested Paul. "I didn't mean to. I got carried away."

Aunt Gabrielle pressed her hand to her forehead. "The important thing is the police have no proof. It's going to be hard for them to build a case. I do wish your father were here to give me his advice! If only I knew where he was! I've left messages everywhere I can think of." Suddenly she turned and left. Ari heard her footsteps running up the servants' staircase.

"Where's she going all of a sudden, I wonder?" Paul asked, glancing after her. "I guess she must be going to try to find out where Dad is."

"I don't know why she wants him," Ari said. "He'll only make things worse."

"I'd be interested in his input," said Paul.

Ari began to feel uneasy being alone with Paul. He stood in the door, blocking her way.

"Hand me a paper towel, will you?" he asked her.

Ari held out a paper towel, but she was careful not to let her hand touch his.

Paul carefully wiped the ink off his fingers. "Look, Ari," he said, "I'm sorry I scared you, okay?"

"I don't want to . . ." She hesitated. "I can't go along with you, do you understand?"

"Why not?" Paul asked softly. "Don't you want us to be together forever?"

"Go away, Paul," Ari whispered, turning away from him. "Please leave me alone."

"You're not ready—that's all. You need time. It's in our blood, though! You're the only one in the family who's not a vampire." He held out his arms. "If you let me make you one, too, we could be close forever."

Ari backed up against the stove. "I'm your alibi," she said steadily, not taking her eyes off his face. "If anything happens to me, the police are going to come looking for you."

"Jeez, Ari." Paul's arms fell to his side. "I'm not going to hurt you. Why do you have to make me feel like some kind of monster? I said I was sorry, didn't I?"

7

He turned away, and a spur of anxiety pricked her. "Where are you going?" she cried.

"Out. It's pretty obvious you don't want me around." He turned around to smile, and she could see the glistening white of his fangs. "Don't worry—I'm not going anyplace you'd want to go." His tone was mocking.

Ari listened until she heard the front door close behind him. She knew that Aunt Gabrielle was still upstairs trying to phone their father. This was her chance.

She quietly tiptoed down the service hall and opened the door to the basement. Until now she had been unable to bring herself to go down the basement stairs. She had tried to avoid even thinking about the boxes stacked down there with her mother's things. The sight of the old toys and the familiar furniture was sure to be painful. But she had no choice. Something was down there that she desperately needed.

CHAPTER
TWO

PAUL WALKED QUICKLY INTO THE NIGHT. THE STREET-lamps of Georgetown were shrouded in mist, and puddles by the curb were crusted with ice. Every catlike step told him that he was a vampire. He let his hand slide along a fence and watched as his fingertips left a trail of phosphorescence. He was scared. The police suspected him of Susannah's murder, and he was in no shape to go to prison. As far as he knew, prisons didn't provide coffins for sleeping.

Paul clenched his hands desperately. Each feast of blood fed a fire inside him that burned with increasing brightness. He was certain he was more a vampire now than ever. Why was he forced to live as a human being? If only Ari would join him.

But he knew he had to keep up the pretense. Ari wasn't ready. He had to go back to school

9

and act like an ordinary student. But it was an empty masquerade. And worse, every day it was getting harder for him to pull off.

Suddenly he froze. A masquerade! In a flash it hit him where he could go for help. His dark eyes glowed with a strange and shifting luminescence as he quickened his pace and turned in the direction of the old C and O Canal.

The row houses along the canal were dark. Only in one did the lights still burn. Outside was a wooden sign that read WILEY HOBAN, COSTUMER AND DESIGNER. Paul smiled. The door had a glass window, but it was curtained with thin white material, so Paul could not see inside. He tried the doorknob.

"We're closed," a voice called out.

Paul rattled the locked door insistently. "It's Paul Montclair, Mr. Hoban. Let me in, will you? It's kind of an emergency."

A bell tinkled and the door opened a crack, revealing a balding, gray-haired man, his face glittering with round glasses. "Gabrielle's nephew?" Mr. Hoban asked. "What do you want at this time of night? Why didn't you phone?"

"It's kind of personal," said Paul, forcing the door open.

Mr. Hoban stepped back in surprise. "I'm already overworked," he protested. "This is my busy season, with all the parties they're having now in Washington. I don't see how I can fit in any more rush jobs."

Paul glanced around the room. The walls

were cluttered with jeweled crowns, felt hats, and rubbery masks—their expressions comically distorted from hanging sagging on long nails.

"This is a special sort of challenge," Paul said. He plucked a rubber mask off the wall and looked at it critically. The material skin seemed even less like human skin than his own. He was sure Mr. Hoban could do better. At Halloween he and Ari had gone into Mr. Hoban's back storeroom and had seen insect costumes, extra-terrestrial creatures—every sort of elaborate fantasy. The man was an artist.

Paul turned around suddenly to face the costume maker. "Make me look human," he demanded.

"But . . ." Mr. Hoban peered at him over his glasses. "I'm not sure I see what you want."

"Look at my eyes!" Paul said, focusing his concentration. He could see the intense lavender glow of his pupils reflected in Mr. Hoban's glasses.

"Remarkable!" exclaimed the costume maker. "How do you do that?" As if he was checking for wires, Mr. Hoban darted a curious glance at Paul's shirt collar.

Paul realized then that it had been a mistake to call attention to his eyes. After all, he could always wear contact lenses to hide them. He didn't need Hoban's help for that.

"My fingernails," he said, holding out his hands and eyeing his glassy nails with dissatisfaction. "If I were a girl, I could wear fingernail

11

polish, but I'm not. I need something that will make them look like regular nails—something that I can paint on."

Mr. Hoban stared at Paul's hands and gulped. "I can't do that."

"Why not?" Paul demanded. "You told me once that you could make me into a silver cream pitcher. What's so hard about changing my fingernails?"

Mr. Hoban blinked. "It's different. That is fantasy, you understand. You wouldn't expect people to believe you were a silver cream pitcher."

Paul grabbed a mirror that lay near the masks and gazed at his face. His heart felt cold like a stone inside him. He had avoided looking into mirrors lately, recoiling when confronted with his own inhuman image. "The skin," he said suddenly. "I need some kind of makeup. I want something that will make me look soft and natural."

Mr. Hoban backed away. "I think you'd better go now," he said.

"Why?" Paul demanded, putting the mirror down and striding toward him. "Aren't you willing to help me out? You call yourself an artist? Aren't you up to the job?"

The old man's face was glistening with sweat as he edged away from Paul. "I do fantasy," he protested weakly. "I tell you, I can't help you."

"Why not?" Paul persisted.

"Because," whispered Mr. Hoban, "this is not

normal! Please leave! Please . . ." He stumbled backward over a small ladder and bit his lip.

A strange feeling swept over Paul at the sight of the blood on Mr. Hoban's lip. His stomach trembled as if he were suddenly going down in a swing.

"Please leave now." Mr. Hoban hastily blotted his lip with his sleeve. Paul stared at the red splotch that had appeared on the white cloth of the shirt. "I have a lot of work to do," Hoban pleaded, his voice squeaky. "Please go!"

Paul sprang swiftly. Throwing his arm around the old man, he pushed Hoban's head back until the veins in his neck bulged and he moaned in fear. Paul sank his teeth into the soft flesh. The costume maker's frail body collapsed, but Paul did not loosen his grip when Hoban fell. With his knee grinding against the wooden floor, Paul ripped the skin and pressed his lips close, sucking hard. The rhythm of Hoban's beating heart forced blood into Paul's throat like a surging fountain. Time stood still. As his sight misted over with red, Paul shivered with pleasure.

At last he rolled away, his face hot and his flesh suffused with blood. He lay for some minutes on the floor, scarcely aware of anything but his own pulsing warmth.

Finally Paul propped himself up on his elbows and glanced at the pathetic body that lay at his feet. Hoban's white apron, glittering with pins, was splashed with silver-dollar-size splotches of blood. There was no doubt that the old man was dead. His chest was perfectly still, and his withered flesh was a ghastly white.

Paul saw that the round glasses lay shattered on the floor. He stood up, dusted off the knees of his jeans, and glanced around anxiously. He couldn't leave Hoban to be found here. The police might make the connection between the old man's death and Susannah's.

Paul went over to the door and pushed the white curtain aside. At least no one seemed to be coming. He returned to the body and swiftly patted Hoban's pockets until he found the key to the shop. Better if the front door were found locked. Otherwise it might look as if Hoban had let in someone he knew and trusted. Paul hesitated a moment, then reached for a rubber mask and slipped it over his face. If anyone were to see him carrying the body, he couldn't be identified.

Hoban was slightly built, but Paul felt the strain in the back of his legs as he hoisted the body over his shoulder. His rubber mask slipped down a bit while he groped for the doorknob. At last he stepped outside and awkwardly locked the door behind him. He realized then that he had left the lights on, but it was too late to go back.

With the body slung awkwardly over his shoulder, Paul made his way down the steps to the canal path. The stupid mask obscured his vision, and the body's weight made him lopsided, but he pressed on until finally he felt the level stone of the path under his feet.

The dark water of the canal gleamed before him. Paul bent over and let the body fall head-first. It slid under the surface with scarcely a splash. He swept the rubber mask off his face and tossed it in, too. It floated for a couple of minutes, its exaggerated features leering up at him mockingly. Then its black eye holes filled with water and it, too, sank below the dark water.

Why did the old man have to say Paul wasn't normal? Even now the hurtful words made him angry. It wouldn't have cost Hoban anything to try to help. Paul was sure he could have, if only he had been willing.

When Paul reached the street, he glanced down and saw that his jacket was spattered with dark drops. He began breathing faster. He tore his jacket off and stuffed it down a storm drain.

Walking quickly now, he turned back toward M Street. He knew he should check to make sure there wasn't any more blood spattered on the rest of his clothes, but he was too agitated to do anything reasonable. A slow-moving Toyota drove toward him, its headlights ablaze. The little car slowed to a crawl, and Paul could see that a frightened girl about his own age was driving. He stepped out into the street and placed his hand on the car's headlight, splaying his fingers over the curved glass. His eyes met hers, and he grinned. She was a pretty brunet, and he wondered with a sudden quiver of excitement what it would be like to pull her out of the car and sink his teeth into her soft flesh. All of a sudden the engine roared, and the car leapt forward, striking Paul a glancing blow that sent him spinning.

He landed on the sidewalk, flat on his face. He was stunned for a moment. He hadn't expected her to gun the engine. Propping himself up with his hands, he turned and angrily watched the Toyota's red taillights disappear into blackness. She could have killed him—if he wasn't already dead.

He realized then that he had better pull himself together, or he was going to do something stupid that would get him in trouble.

Suddenly he was sick with bitterness. Before, he'd thought he could count on his family, but none of them was much use. Plainly Ari was afraid of him. Aunt Gabrielle was a bundle of nerves, and his father, as usual, was missing just when he was needed most.

Paul got up and continued on to M Street. The lights there were bright, and Paul glanced down anxiously at his shoes, checking to make sure they weren't caked with blood. Just then he heard a girl's voice call his name.

"Paul! What are you doing out? I thought you were sick!"

Paul spun around to see Sybil Barron coming toward him. "I had to get out of the house," he said.

"You poor thing," Sybil cried, shifting a bag of groceries to her other hip. Her frizzy red hair stood out like a halo around her head, and her eyes were moist with sympathy. "I'm so, so sorry about poor Susannah. It must be just awful for you."

Paul felt tears sting his eyes. He had liked Susannah a lot. In his own mind he thought of her death as a tragic accident. He felt real grief, as if it had been a stranger who had killed her.

"If there's anything I can do . . ." Sybil said awkwardly.

"Thanks," he muttered.

"It'll be better when you're over the flu," she said. "Then you won't have so much time think about it. Have you gotten a blood test, in case it turns out to be mono?"

Paul gulped. He wished she hadn't mentioned blood. "I don't think it's mono. I'm sure it's only the flu. But if it hangs on much longer, I'll get it checked out."

Sybil smiled. "It seems like you're never around lately. A couple of times my brother Rab has said he'd like to meet you. But last time he was here, you were sick."

"I'm better now," Paul said. "It's just that this stuff with Susannah's been . . . an awful blow."

Sybil nodded sympathetically.

Paul watched as she headed to a car down the street and got in. She shot him a tearful smile before driving away. All at once Paul began to feel better. Sybil's crush on him used to embarrass him, but it didn't anymore. Now it suggested all sorts of intriguing possibilities.

What he particularly liked was the way she wasn't afraid of him at all.

Ari put her mother's candelabra on either side of her, then placed a pair of candlesticks on a chest that stood at the foot of the bed. Soon all the candles were burning, and her bedroom was flooded with a flickering, uncertain light. She wasn't sure how long they would last. Hopefully until dawn. These candles, which had been buried in the basement with the rest of her mother's belongings, were the only ones in the house.

Now, of course, Ari understood why Aunt Gabrielle wouldn't allow fire in her house. But it was one of the things that she had found particularly strange at first. The silver candelabra in Aunt Gabrielle's dining room had tiny glass bulbs. Even the logs in the living-room fireplace were electric.

Ari glanced around her bedroom, wondering how she could possibly expect to sleep when she was trembling with fear. Both of her doors were bolted from the inside, but the doors could be kicked in. The small flames around the bed gave her little feeling of security.

Finally her eyes fell on a large chessboard folded in a corner of the room. She had found the chessboard in the same packing box as the candelabra and had been strangely drawn to it.

She wasn't sure why. Paul had been the one who liked to play chess when they were younger. Maybe it was because the black-and-white checkered design of the board was the same as the marble floor of Aunt Gabrielle's long hallway. She unfolded it on the bed and set each piece in its square—knight, bishop, pawn.

Looking at the chessboard now, Ari felt vaguely disturbed. The pieces wobbled, jarred by her movement on the bed. She reached out to steady them but suddenly jerked her hand away as if she'd been burned.

The pieces were alive.

Standing on the chessboard was a tiny version of Sybil, her frizzy red hair standing out on her head. She was wearing neat little boots and a long black skirt and a puffy-sleeved, calico print shirt that went narrow at the wrist. Ari's boyfriend, Cos, only three inches tall, sneezed into a tiny tissue. The tiny human chess pieces began scurrying around the board like a swarm of insects, more and more of them appearing by the second, until Ari was dizzy looking at them. Kids from school carried their brightly colored book bags as they sped around the squares. Ari caught a glimpse of Jessie's blond hair in the confusion of tiny figures. There was Paul! And her father in a small black cape. Ari watched in amazement as they leapfrogged and occasionally stumbled around the board, picking themselves up and running in furious, meaningless motion. She thought about upending the board and

19

dumping them off of it, but she couldn't bring herself to touch it. Slowly she realized that they were all moving in a circle—it was a whirlpool, and they were being drawn into the vortex!

"No!" cried Ari, panic seizing her. "Stop!"

A chess piece fell over with a clunk. All at once the tiny people vanished, and in their place were the original dusty bishops and pawns standing neatly in their appointed squares. Except one. Ari blinked. A pawn had toppled over. She stared at it in horror. *Someone else is going to die!*

CHAPTER
THREE

THE PHONE RANG IN RAB BARRON'S APARTMENT IN Charlottesville. He picked it up with a feeling of dark foreboding.

"Hullo?"

"Rab? It's Sybil. How are you?"

"I'm fine, Syb. What is it?" He frowned. "Is anything wrong?"

"Can't I just call to say hello? Listen, you remember that boy that I mentioned to you that I sort of liked, but it was no good, because he was going with somebody else? Well, I think he sort of likes me now."

"That's great." Rab hesitated. "Are you sure nothing's wrong?"

"Well, nothing *new* has happened. You already know about poor Susannah being killed."

Rab swallowed. He had been at the mall that afternoon with Sybil and her friends when they

21

had learned about Susannah's brutal murder. It was the same day he had met Ari. *Ari!* Suddenly an inexplicable bolt of fear shot through him. "Is Ari okay?" he asked sharply.

"She's sad, naturally, about what happened to Susannah. Why are you so worried about Ari?"

"I don't know. I keep having this weird feeling—I can't explain it."

There was a short silence. Then Sybil said, "I wonder if it's because I got my braces off."

"What?"

"I mean the reason why this boy noticed me," Sybil explained patiently. "Maybe it's like in those old movies when the girl takes off her glasses, and suddenly the guy realizes how beautiful she is."

Rab smiled. Sybil obviously had other things on her mind. "Maybe he realized what an interesting person you are."

"I don't want to be an interesting person," said Sybil. "I want to be beautiful like Ari. I want to be a femme fatale, one of those women who make men drop things and stumble whenever they see them."

"It sounds embarrassing," said Rab. "I don't think you'd like it."

"I'd like it, all right," said Sybil gloomily. "I just wish I had a chance to try it. If only I thought there was even a tiny chance that I might develop into a femme fatale when I get a little older . . . I wonder what I'd look like if I straightened my hair. . . ."

"I gotta go, Syb," said Rab hastily. He was in

no mood to listen to the endless pros and cons on the question of straightening Sybil's hair. "I've got a whole mess of work to do."

But after Rab hung up the phone, he found it impossible to work. His concentration was shot. It was a cold night, but he threw a window open, hoping the fresh air would clear his mind. The wind brushed a leafy branch against the screen, and he felt uneasy.

He sat down at his desk, staring sightlessly at his history book. It was hopeless. He slapped the book shut suddenly and reached for a pack of cards. When he was a kid, he had gotten someone to show him how to shuffle the way river-boat gamblers did. For some reason it drove his mother crazy.

He cut the deck and shuffled with a sudden blur of cascading cards. Then he laid out a game of solitaire. He drew a card and played it. The next card was the ace of spades. He glanced down. The ace of spades was already on the table. Strange. Holding his breath, he drew another card. Ace of spades. His heart began galloping in his chest. He glanced at the cards on the table. All black aces. He jumped up suddenly, knocking over his chair.

"Something's wrong with Ari," he said aloud.

As if in answer to his question, a sudden draft scattered the cards, blowing several onto the floor.

Rab slammed the window shut. Without pausing to retrieve the cards, he reached for his jacket and car keys. Even though he had given

23

up smoking before college, he felt an urgent need for a cigarette.

He hurried downstairs, his breath making little puffs of white in the cold darkness. He ran across the dark parking lot and jumped in his car. What he was doing made no sense, and he knew it. But that didn't stop him. He *had* to go back to Washington. He drove by a convenience store and bought a pack of cigarettes.

As he pulled onto the highway, he struck a match and lit up. Ari's face appeared before him—a flimsy, shifting image. Her hair was a mass of darkness, and her mouth was open in a horrified scream. As suddenly as she had appeared, she was gone. Rab felt a sharp pain and looked down in surprise to see that the match had singed his fingers. He tossed it out the window.

Highway 29 was dark, and there was hardly any traffic. From inside the car the night seemed still and calm. Still, Rab's skin felt as if it had been scraped by sandpaper and all the nerves had been exposed. He wished he could have been honest with Ari the time he had had a chance to talk to her. He flexed his fingers nervously on the steering wheel. But the secret he was keeping wasn't his alone—that was what held him back.

He couldn't believe that Ari and Sybil had become friends. What an irony! He had nearly burst out laughing when his mother told him. It was convenient in a way, but in another way it couldn't have been more awkward. Sybil was

24

constantly hinting at him to ask Ari out. Rab shook his head.

All of a sudden a tall black figure loomed ahead of him. Rab jabbed his foot on the brake. The tires shrieked as he skidded to a stop only a few feet short of the man.

Rab leapt out of the car. "What do you think you're doing standing in the middle of the road?" he yelled. "I almost hit you."

The stranger was standing directly in front of the headlights. His skin was bleached by the glare. Rab could see that he had strongly marked black eyebrows and glossy black hair. Oddly enough, he was wearing a cape. Rab glanced down at his feet, recognizing the look of hand-made shoes. Expensive clothes. He guessed the man had probably blown a tire on his Mercedes or something like that.

"I'm sorry I frightened you," the man said softly, "but I have wrecked my car, and I have the most urgent need to get to Washington at once. I wonder if you could give me a lift."

Rab hesitated. Without waiting for an answer, the tall man got in the car. Rab felt his face getting hot. Obviously he had made a mistake not locking the doors. Now it looked as if he had, against his will, picked up a hitchhiker.

He got back in the car and took a deep drag off his cigarette. It had been so long since he'd smoked that inhaling made him feel sick to his stomach. This was obviously going to be one of those nights when everything went wrong. If he

Ari didn't catch half of what Sybil said after that. Numbness stole over her as her friend described their various classmates' horror at the news of Susannah's death.

At last something Sybil said caught Ari's attention. "Amanda told me there wasn't any blood!"

Hot alarm surged through Ari's brain.

"She said Susannah's throat was cut," Sybil went on, "but there wasn't a drop of blood on the sheets. Amanda says the burglars must have slit her throat in the bathtub and washed away the blood, then carried her body to the bed. That's the only possible explanation. Isn't that awful? I can't bear to think of it. I keep telling myself that Amanda got it wrong."

Ari glanced at the kitchen door and saw her aunt staring at her silently, her lavender eyes pulsing with an unearthly glow. She signaled Ari to hang up by making a quick slashing motion across her throat.

Ari winced at the graphic gesture.

"Don't tell Paul what I said." Sybil lowered her voice almost to a whisper. "I mean about the blood and all. There's got to be some other explanation."

There is another explanation, thought Ari, feeling a hysterical giggle well up in her throat. *Only, I can't tell you.*

"I'm getting a lot of static," Sybil complained. "Can you hear it? This connection is terrible."

"We'd better hang up," Ari said quickly.

4

weren't careful, he would probably end up wrecking his own car. Rab clamped the cigarette tightly in his mouth. "I'll take you far enough that you can phone for help," he said.

"Is it—forgive me—absolutely necessary that you smoke?" the stranger asked.

"Yes," snapped Rab. He felt remorseful as soon as the words were out of his mouth. His passenger was very pale. Perhaps he had been injured when he had wrecked his car. He might even be in shock. "You aren't hurt, are you?" Rab asked, glancing at him. "I mean, you didn't get banged up in the wreck or anything, did you?"

The man raised his dark eyebrows so that the slope of his high cheekbones was even more prominent. "Oh, no," he said. "I'm perfectly all right, thank you." He glared at Rab disapprovingly. "It's only that I'm allergic to cigarette smoke."

"Open the window, then," said Rab. He stubbed out his cigarette and at once struck a match to light another. The brief flame from the match cast a lurid orange glow on the stranger's odd, pale face. The man pressed against the window, staring at the flame with wide eyes, as if Rab had pulled a gun on him instead of simply lighting a cigarette. What was this guy's problem? If he didn't like the smoke, he could get out of the car. Nobody had asked him to get in.

Rab sucked deeply on the cigarette, regarding its glowing tip with misgiving. He knew that he would pay for it tomorrow with a headache. It wasn't that he was going to start smok-

26

ing again, he reminded himself. He had kicked the habit for good and would throw the pack away as soon as he got to the city. It was only that he needed to calm his nerves tonight.

He stole another glance at the elegantly dressed man beside him. The stranger was staring at the gearshift of the car with a frown. "I don't know how to drive a stick shift," he said.

The man's tone made Rab nervous. If he had known how, would he have tried to steal the car?

Suddenly Rab saw a sign for a small town— Madison. He stopped the car abruptly. "You get out here," he said. "You can phone for help nearby."

Anger flared in the stranger's dark eyes. Some trick of the light made them look as if a fire were lit inside them. He opened his mouth, then stopped. To Rab's relief he got out of the car. "Thank you," he said softly. "I appreciate your help."

Rab looked back as he drove off and caught a glimpse of the stranger's beak-nosed face glowing red in the car's taillights. Rab was not used to being intimidated, but the stranger had been fully as tall as he was and looked powerfully built. Worse, he had the oily, sinister manner of a criminal. Rab shivered. Seldom had he been so glad to put space between him and another person, he thought. He gunned the motor. What a night!

CHAPTER FOUR

A LIGHT TAPPING SOUNDED ON ARI'S DOOR. "ARI? Ari, darling? Are you asleep?" It was only Aunt Gabrielle. Ari sighed with relief as she unlocked the bolts. The candles flickered and smoked when she flung the door open.

"Ari!" Aunt Gabrielle gasped at the sight of the flames. She stepped back at once, a look of horror on her face.

"I'm sorry," cried Ari. "I forgot." She hastily blew out the candles.

Aunt Gabrielle stepped into Ari's room, fanning her face with her hand. "My dear, that burned smell—I don't see how you can stand it." She gazed in bewilderment at the barricade of candles. "What is this all about?"

Ari was suddenly ashamed. Her aunt had tried so hard to be kind—it would be terrible if she thought that the candles were meant for her.

"It's Paul!" Ari cried. "He wants to make me be a vampire. I keep worrying that he's going to break in here while I'm asleep. . . ." Ari couldn't go on.

"Oh, my poor dear." Aunt Gabrielle cupped Ari's face in her thin, pale hands and gazed solicitously into her eyes. Ari knew the gesture was meant to be comforting, but she felt herself go cold at her aunt's bony touch. "I'm sure that now that he realizes you don't want that, he won't insist," Aunt Gabrielle murmured. "Paul loves you, dearest!"

Choking on a sob, Ari pulled away from her. "He kept saying it was for my own good. He said we'd be closer if I were a vampire, and I could live forever." She fell onto her bed. "I don't want to live forever. I don't even know what he's thinking anymore. He's like a stranger."

"Communication is the key, Ari," said Aunt Gabrielle softly. "You must talk to Paul and make him understand how you feel."

Ari swallowed her bitter laughter. To hear Aunt Gabrielle sounding like a self-help book would have been funny if the situation had not been so desperate. Maybe Paul *had* given up on making her into a vampire. But how could she be sure?

Aunt Gabrielle's head jerked. "Did you hear that? Someone's at the door." She frowned. "Who can it possibly be at this late hour? Do you imagine Paul forgot his key? I'd better go see." She paused at the door and smiled. "By the way, I was coming in to tell you that I did at last succeed in reaching your father. He was in Charlottesville. He said he'd come at once."

Ari felt a sick clutch in her stomach. "Maybe that's him now."

"Oh, no, dear. It can't be," Aunt Gabrielle said serenely as she walked out of Ari's room. "Richard always comes in the back way."

Ari felt as tense as a stretched rubber band until she heard quick steps outside her door.

A moment later her aunt returned. "It's a young man for you, dear," Aunt Gabrielle said. "I didn't want to tell him that this was no time to be calling. I wasn't sure whether you wanted to see him or not."

"Is it Cos?" cried Ari, clutching her hand to her chest in alarm.

Aunt Gabrielle shook her head. "He said his name was Rab."

Rab! Ari ran downstairs. She found Sybil's brother waiting for her in the hall. She was always startled at how he resembled Sybil and yet was so unlike her. His hair was crinkly like Sybil's, and he had her high-arched brows, but while her eyebrows were a soft strawberry-blond, his were black. He had a strong, hooked nose and a solid jaw, which tonight looked grimly set. To her surprise he was smoking.

Ari stared at him. "I didn't realize that you smoked," she said.

Rab took the cigarette from his mouth and stared at it for a moment. "I've given it up." He cracked the door and pitched it outside. Ari saw it cartwheel into the darkness.

"I'm about to jump out of my skin," complained Rab. He glanced around the dim hallway. "Let's go get a cup of coffee. Do you think your aunt will mind?"

Ari shook her head. "Let me get my coat."

She was relieved to have an excuse to leave the house. Paul would be returning any minute. She glanced at Rab. "What's going on? I thought you had gone back to Charlottesville."

"I had," he said. Ari got into Rab's car and slammed the door shut. "Only thing is, I got a funny feeling that something was wrong." He took a deep breath as he slid in behind the wheel. "The next thing I knew, I was driving back here."

Ari fell silent. Could Rab possibly know about what had happened to Paul? "You heard about Susannah being murdered," she said at last. "That was horrible."

Rab shook his head. "I didn't even know Susannah, so it couldn't be that." He glanced at her with an odd, fearful look in his eyes. "Ari, do you ever have visions?"

Ari stared, unable to speak.

"Saint Teresa of Avila had visions," Rab went on quickly, turning his attention back to the road. "And Joan of Arc. You can check that out."

"That was a long time ago," Ari finally managed to say.

"Well, it doesn't matter. Forget I even mentioned visions." Rab shrugged. "Let's say I had a premonition. Something told me I'd better check on you."

Ari forced herself to smile. "As you can see, I'm fine."

"What about Paul?" He glanced at her quickly. "Is he okay, too?"

Ari's eyes flickered away from him. "Sure," she said colorlessly. "I think he's pretty much over that flu he had."

Rab pulled into the parking lot of a doughnut shop, and they got out. Ari shivered at the sudden cold and thrust her freezing hands into the pockets of her coat.

Had Rab been trying to tell her just now that *he* had had a vision? she wondered. A vision about her and Paul perhaps? If so, she didn't want to hear about it. She was sick of visions, visions that haunted her and made her life a torment. Already she was regretting the impulse that had made her come out with Rab tonight.

The doughnut shop smelled strong of coffee. It felt good to get out of the cold, and Ari immediately slipped out of her coat. Several customers at the counter were glumly hunched over their cups. Ari got decaf and a filled doughnut, and she and Rab sat down in a booth.

Ari bit into her doughnut and brushed the powdered sugar off her face. "I love lemon-filled doughnuts," she said. "Actually, I love food."

"That's good." Rab grinned. "Since it's necessary for life, I mean."

Ari blinked at him, remembering that Aunt Gabri, Paul, and her father never ate at all. But then, why would they? They weren't alive.

"Did I say something wrong?" asked Rab, looking at her.

She shook her head.

"I never know where I am with you," he said. "You never tell me what's on your mind. Talking to you is like walking through a room with the lights off. I keep bumping into things."

"That's nice. Thank you."

"Don't be sarcastic. I'm only trying to help. Jeez, I feel like an idiot." Rab ran his fingers through his hair. "I drive all this way in the middle of the night, and now you're telling me everything's just fine." His color changed. "I nearly ran down some guy that had wrecked his car. It was a close thing. I was lucky I didn't kill him."

Ari could see that he was shaken. "What happened?" she asked, eyeing him anxiously.

A shadow passed across Rab's face. "Nothing, really. He jumped in my car without even asking permission, and then he insisted that I take him into the city."

It sounded like the sort of thing Ari's father would do. She recalled his high-handed, dictatorial manner, and something clicked in her mind. Hadn't Aunt Gabrielle said she had reached her father in Charlottesville? That was where Rab went to school! Ari shook her head. Her imagination was running wild.

33

"I only took him as far as the next little town," Rab went on. "Then I made him get out. To tell you the truth, something about him gave me the creeps."

"What did he look like?" Ari's throat felt constricted. She was sure she already knew what he looked like.

"Why do you want to know?" Rab gave her a piercing look.

"I was wondering if it could have been my father," Ari admitted. "He was staying in Charlottesville—and I know he was on his way up here. He's tall. Over six feet. Black, curly hair. Pale, with a sort of hook nose. Well-dressed."

"Yes," whispered Rab. "That's him."

Ari looked at him in silence.

Rab had gone pale. "I nearly ran him down, Ari. I could have killed him."

Ari smiled bitterly. "Don't worry. He's indestructible. Haven't you heard that only the good die young?"

Rab didn't respond.

"I'm afraid of him," she went. "You can't imagine what it's like to have a father like he is. We never know what he's going to do next. And the worst part . . ." She choked up and couldn't go on.

"Yes?" asked Rab gently. "What's the worst part?"

Ari dabbed at her eyes with a napkin. "Sometimes I think Paul takes after him—just a

34

little. Don't tell Sybil I said that, please."

"No. No, of course not." Rab's eyes were troubled.

Neither of them said anything for a long time. Ari forced herself to eat the rest of her doughnut. She was embarrassed. Somehow she always ended up saying more to Rab than she had intended.

Rab smiled. "'Separated by the river of our common blood.'"

Ari stared at him. "Why do you say that?" Her mouth had gone dry.

"It's a line from a book." Rab looked sheepish. "It's true, though, isn't it? People from the same family are so alike sometimes that it takes your breath away. But they stand looking at each other as if they were strangers. I notice it all the time."

Ari wished they hadn't started talking about families. Why did Rab always make her feel uncomfortable? "Did you realize that my dad went out with your mother when they were in high school?" she asked suddenly.

"Yeah," he said in a strangled voice. "I knew that."

Ari's eyes met his. "Now that you've met him, can you see it? I just can't imagine it, can you?"

"No." Rab shook his head. "I can't."

"He's certainly different from the man she married." Ari thought of Mr. Barron. "Your dad is nice. He seems very reliable."

"He's a corporate lawyer." Rab smiled. "So I

guess reliable is just what you would expect. Reliable and boring."

"Boring is not all bad. I wish my father were more like him. Has your mother ever told you anything about my dad?"

"What do you mean?" His eyes shifted uneasily.

"I thought she might have confided in you more than she did in Sybil," said Ari. "Since you're the oldest."

"I got the idea things were pretty serious between them," Rab said. "Is that the kind of thing you mean?"

"I guess."

"She was kind of bitter, I think," he went on. "I don't know how to take a lot of what she said."

"What exactly did she say?"

Rab hesitated.

"Go ahead," said Ari. "You aren't going to hurt my feelings. I hate him already."

"I got the idea she thought he wasn't quite . . . normal," said Rab.

Ari gazed at Rab in blank surprise. She was taken aback by how much it hurt for him to say that out loud. Paul had been right—they could never get away from the fact that Richard was their father. It was as if he was a part of them in some way that they couldn't escape, no matter how much they wanted to.

"She was just spouting off," said Rab. "I guess I shouldn't have said that."

"No," said Ari. "I asked you to." She swallowed. "Don't you think it's funny that your mother fell in love with him, considering she felt that way about him." She smiled wryly. "Or is that one of those things I'm going to understand better when I get older?"

"I don't think anybody understands love," offered Rab.

"I certainly don't. People change a lot. That must be what happens. One day a person is sweet—wonderful—and the next day they're completely different, just as if somebody pulled a switch. One minute it's light, and the next it's dark."

"I don't believe that," said Rab.

"Believe it," said Ari bleakly. "Nothing else explains how people like my mother and your mother could have fallen in love with a man like my father."

"People are complex, that's all. They have different sides to their personalities," Rab said. "I don't believe it works the way you say. That would mean everyone is completely unpredictable."

"People *are* completely unpredictable."

"I think you need some sleep." Rab looked down at his long fingers. "I do, too, for that matter. I wish I hadn't smoked all those stupid cigarettes."

He was silent as he drove Ari home, and she was glad. It was a relief not to have to make conversation.

37

"I wish you'd come spend the weekend in Charlottesville with me sometime," Rab said when they pulled up in front of the house.

"I don't think Cos would like that."

"Tell Cos we're only friends," said Rab. "It's the truth." Ari followed his eyes as he glanced up at the lighted windows of Aunt Gabrielle's town house. The rest of the street was dark. At this late hour, only the Montclair family was awake. "I could show you around the university," he said. "You can think about whether you'd like to go to school there. You won't be living here in your aunt's house forever, you know."

Ari looked at him in surprise. She realized suddenly that she had lost her capacity to imagine the future, and she shivered.

"Are you okay?" Rab asked quickly.

Ari closed her eyes. "Quit asking me if I'm okay! Leave me alone!" She flung open the car door and ran up the steps.

Tears welled in her eyes as she let herself in the front door. Then she froze. She could hear a voice coming from upstairs. It was her father!

CHAPTER
FIVE

RICHARD MONTCLAIR PACED AROUND PAUL'S ROOM restlessly, then suddenly stopped. "What was that?" he asked sharply.

"It's Ari. I wonder where she's been." Paul's face darkened. "Probably out with Cos."

"Cos?" Richard snorted. "That's not even a name."

"He's Ari's boyfriend. You met him, remember? At the bar that night you jumped Jessie?"

"Oh, him." Richard dismissed Cos with an abrupt gesture. "Where were you when I got here? Gabri had no idea."

"I was out." Paul propped his feet up on his desk and linked his fingers behind his neck. Funny how his father didn't scare him anymore. He felt as if they were on an equal footing.

"It would be helpful," Richard said in measured tones, "if you would tell your aunt where you're going and when you'll be back."

"Yeah," he said, smiling. "But I don't always want Aunt Gabri to know where I'm going."

Richard stiffened. "Where exactly were you? Where was it that you couldn't tell Gabri?"

"I went to see a man about a disguise," Paul said. "But it didn't work out. I had to kill him."

"Not somebody that you know, Paul?"

"Not a friend or anything," Paul admitted reluctantly. "If you've got to know—it was that old guy who made costumes for Aunt Gabri."

Richard's eyes were closed, but their glow shone through his eyelids, giving a startling luminous quality to the whiteness of his flesh. "Never kill people that you know. Do you hear me? It leads to awkward questions."

Paul grinned. "What is this? A sermon? Let me get my hymn book, okay?"

Richard took an angry step toward him, but Paul only laughed. "What are you going to do?" he taunted. "Beat me up? Kill me?"

"You can't go on like this, Paul." Richard spoke urgently. "You're already in trouble. The police are on your trail. If you keep this up, you're going to bring disaster down on all of us."

Paul shook his head. "You make me sick. You do what you want, then you come here and boss me around. Well, forget it. I'll do what I want, and you can't stop me."

Richard's eyes narrowed to glittering slits. "You're young. You don't have any control over your appetite. You've become a vampire far too soon."

"Kind of too late to worry about that now, isn't it?" Paul was surprised at how much he enjoyed baiting his father. He was getting revenge, he supposed, for all the years his father had ignored him.

"So, what are you going to do next?" demanded Richard.

Paul hesitated. "I . . . I guess I'll go on with what I'm doing. Go to school and all that. Like Aunt Gabri says, the cops don't have any evidence. I'll be okay."

"Passing as human takes enormous self-control," said his father. "You have to constantly be on guard against your nature. It's endless self-denial. It's impossible!"

"You're making too big a deal out of it," said Paul. "Fuss, fuss, fuss—that's all you and Gabri do."

Suddenly Richard slapped him.

Paul held his hand to his stinging cheek. Hot rage flashed through him. He leapt up and his hands were around his father's neck, choking him. The older man fell under him, and Paul felt a surge of exultation. Then all at once he felt a blow to the stomach, and his father was on top. Paul's head rang as his father slapped him again and again. The heavier man's weight pinned Paul to the floor, and a bony knee ground into his chest.

When at last the blows stopped, Paul found

himself looking into the dark, shimmering eyes of his father.

"Is this a sample of your self-control?" Richard asked venomously. Taking a deep breath, he struggled to his feet and extended a hand to Paul.

Paul took his father's hand and got up, a bit breathless. "You made me mad, hitting me like that."

"Somebody's always going to be making you mad," said Richard. "That's the way it goes."

How could his father be scolding him for having a short fuse after what Paul had seen of *his* violent temper? He started to say so but thought better of it. His head was still ringing.

Richard began pulling on his gloves as if nothing had happened. He wasn't even out of breath. Only his tousled black locks showed there had been any fight. "Come with me," he suggested.

"Come with you? You mean, now?" asked Paul, surprised.

"Yes, now." Richard smoothed his dark hair back with his hand. "Come live with me as a vampire."

Paul hesitated. "I can't leave Ari."

Richard shrugged. "We can take her with us."

"She won't go." Paul glanced at the closed door between their rooms. "And I can't leave without her."

"Come for a few days, then. You can always come back here when you want."

42

"Really?" Paul glanced at Ari's door. It was an attractive offer—getting away from his troubles for a few days. No homework. No hassles with the police. "Okay," he said at last. "You're on."

Ari had trembled when she'd heard the thud of falling bodies in Paul's bedroom, but she had been too afraid to open the door. Now it was quiet, and that was almost worse. The stillness was terrifying. Sitting up in bed, surrounded by flickering candles, she stared blankly at the moving shadows on her walls and ceiling.

"It's time," said a quiet voice behind her. "You are ready." Ari spun around, but no one was there. Her heart raced. Suddenly her room was full of confused voices. Her lampshade fell askew, and she gasped as a hawk swooped low over her bed, huge and heavy. He landed awkwardly on the top of her wardrobe, and his glittering eyes regarded her with a look of unnerving intelligence. His raptor profile was silhouetted against the white wall, and she realized his beak was red—glistening with blood.

Ari put her pillow over her head. She was stifled by the pillow's weight, and cotton fibers tickled her nose. Her head was hot; she could barely breathe, but at least she could no longer hear the desperate fluttering of wings. Her tears wet the pillow, and she wept until at last the oblivion of sleep closed over her.

* * *

43

When Ari woke, sunlight flooded in the window. A burnt waxy smell filled the room. She saw that the candles had all sputtered out in their sockets. Suddenly she remembered that her father had been here last night.

"Paul!" she cried. She flung the connecting door open, but even before she saw that the room was empty, she knew Paul was gone. The house was ominously silent, and his coffin was pushed under his bed.

Ari bolted downstairs and found a brief note attached to the refrigerator with a magnet:

Paul has gone to stay with Richard for a few days, darling. Please, don't worry.

Aunt Gabrielle

Sunlight beamed strongly in the dining-room windows, stirring the chandelier prisms into a fiery brilliance and pointing to a few white motes of dust on the table. Ari had a hundred questions for Aunt Gabrielle, but she knew it was no use. Her aunt was now tightly closed in her coffin.

CHAPTER
SIX

"ARI!" SYBIL CRIED. "WAIT UP!"

Ari had been heading toward the Schuler Building when she heard her friend's voice. "Paul's not coming to school today?" Sybil panted, skidding to a stop next to her.

"No," said Ari. "He's gone to stay with our father a few days."

Sybil nodded. "It'll do him good to get away to where he's not always reminded of Susannah." She gave Ari a sideways glance. "Where does your dad live, anyway?"

"I'm not sure," said Ari. Feeling Sybil's curious eyes on her, she added, "I went to bed early—before they left. So I didn't get all the details."

"I thought you and Paul weren't going to have anything to do with your dad," Sybil said. "Did he and Paul make up?"

"I guess," said Ari desperately. "I'm really not sure."

"I ran into Paul last night when I was coming out of the grocery store." Sybil blushed self-consciously. "He said he wasn't feeling too well, but since he was up and around, I was hoping he might get back to school today."

Ari stared at her in alarm. She wanted to scream, "Don't like my brother, Sybil. Stay away from him!" Instead, she merely repeated numbly, "You ran into Paul?"

Sybil nodded. "I was coming out of Dean and DeLuca. My mother has gotten to where she won't go to get groceries at all. It must be some new kind of phobia. These days she either has them delivered or she makes Dad or me go for them. It's very strange."

Ari had a good idea why Mrs. Barron didn't want to go near Dean and DeLuca. It was probably there that she had run into Richard.

"I could tell Paul was really broken up about Susannah," Sybil went on. "He was so pale. I know it was a dreadful shock. You didn't tell him about what Amanda said about the blood, did you?"

Ari jumped. "No," she said hastily. "Don't worry." Ari wondered if Sybil was aware that Rab had returned to town late last night. Probably not, or she would have mentioned it. Ari was still unclear on Rab's motivation for coming, and she felt uncomfortable about it. She remembered her vision about the converging chess pieces.

Already Rab's path had crossed with her father's. It couldn't be a good sign.

"Ari!" a boy's voice yelled.

Cos! She ran to him and buried her nose against his chest.

"Things are bad at home, huh?" he murmured, enfolding her in his arms.

"The police came last night and asked Paul a bunch of questions," she said. "He's really upset. He's gone to stay with our dad."

"Poor guy," said Cos. "I guess he's not up to going to the funeral tomorrow, then."

Ari shook her head.

"They're going to close school so we all can go," put in Sybil. Everywhere Ari looked, she saw faces that were sober and shocked. Susannah's death had put a blanket of gloom over St. Anselm's. Ari shot an uneasy glance up at Cos's face. She loved his untidy brown hair and the sunlit flecks in his brown eyes. She drew close to him and held him tight.

"Let's go on in and sit in the commons," Cos suggested. "All anybody can talk about out here is murder, and I've had about all I can take of that."

Ari nodded. She was terrified whenever Susannah's name was mentioned, sure that somehow she would give herself away.

Cos put his arm around Ari as they walked inside the building. An open arch separated the commons room from the main hallway. Ari had never seen the fireplace lit, but it contained charred logs. A brightly colored heraldic shield hung over the mantel, and the room's walls were decorated with photographs of sports teams from long ago.

Cos fell into a huge leather chair that had its back to the door and pulled Ari down onto his lap. "At last," he whispered, "we can be alone!"

She stroked his untidy hair, loving its faint, indefinable scent. Cos was so right for her, she thought. His high spirits were like a lucky charm against the dark shadows of her other world—the vampire world that threatened to engulf her. Ari felt a spreading warmth reach her toes as they kissed.

"Hardly any blood was left in her," someone said.

Suddenly Ari went rigid. Cos mouthed, "Jessie," and signaled to her to be quiet. Then she heard Nadia's high-pitched voice. But Nadia spoke so softly that Ari couldn't quite make out the words.

She needed no urging from Cos to keep her still. Jessie frightened her. She knew he thought there was something strange about Paul.

"Amanda said her throat was cut," Ari heard Nadia saying. It sounded as if the two had drawn closer.

"I think they cut her throat to cover up what really happened," muttered Jessie.

"What?" Nadia said. "You mean that you think Paul used a knife on her so nobody would suspect he's a vampire?"

"Yeah, but he couldn't fool me," said Jessie.

Ari's eyes widened. Somehow Jessie had guessed what had happened! He and Nadia both knew Paul was a vampire! She froze in horror.

Cos must have sensed her panic. He held his finger to his lips and put his hand lightly over Ari's mouth to signal silence. Ari could only hope that Nadia and Jessie wouldn't discover them. It was too late now to reveal themselves.

"Think about it, Nadia," Jessie continued. "It's the only thing that makes sense. Amanda's idea that burglars cut Susannah's throat over a bathtub is stupid. Why would burglars want to do something like that? It's not like they're worried about messing up the carpet."

"Oh, Jessie, I'm so scared," whimpered Nadia.

"Don't worry," said Jessie. "I'm going to fix Paul Montclair so he'll never kill anybody again."

Ari could not still an involuntary jerk of alarm. She wished she knew what Cos was thinking.

"You can bet that sister of his is in it up to her eyeballs, too," Jessie added.

"I know she is," said Nadia. "She always backs away from me real fast when I make the sign of the cross. I'm sure she's a vampire. She's worse than he is. I just wish we had some solid information about what they're up to."

"I've got it all figured out," said Jessie. "I'll lie in wait outside their house, and if any one of them comes out after dark, I'll follow them and see what they're up to. If they're vampires, they've got to have blood, right? All I've got to do is catch them in the act."

"It sounds too dangerous!" cried Nadia. "What if something happens to you, Jessie!"

"Nothing's going to happen to me," said Jessie casually. "Of course, I may have to kill them."

Ari didn't hear Nadia's response. Their voices became fainter and fainter until they were inaudible. The sounds of feet shuffling in the hall outside the commons room told them it was nearly time for class. Ari sighed deeply.

Cos stared at her, his eyes bulging in shock.

Ari struggled to smile. "I guess that makes it official. Jessie is out of his mind."

Cos leapt up from the deep leather chair so fast that Ari had to grab hold of the chair's arm to keep from falling. "How can you joke about it, Ari?" Cos cried. "Jessie's got a bunch of guns, and he's talking about killing you!"

Ari gulped. "We're going to be late for class."

Cos stared at her as if she had gone insane. He laid his hand on her shoulder and spoke gently. "I'm going to the counseling office right now and get help. You be careful while I'm gone."

"What are you going to tell them?"

"The truth. Now promise me you're going to stay out of Jessie's way. Your first class is calculus, isn't it?"

Ari nodded miserably.

"That's good. Jessie's first-period class is in the other wing." Cos's face darkened. "I don't think he's got a gun here at school, but don't take any chances. Jeez, I can't believe this. It's too horrible to think about."

After Cos left, Ari realized that Cos's going to the authorities frightened her more than anything Jessie had said. She knew Jessie couldn't hurt Paul or Aunt Gabrielle—not by shooting at them, anyway. But the more people heard Jessie's talk about vampires, the more people might begin to suspect the truth.

At lunch Ari stared at her plate, her appetite gone. The morning had passed in a haze of sick anxiety. She wished now that she had gone to the office with Cos. At least then she would have had some clue about what was going on. As it was, all she could do was wait and imagine the worst.

Sybil squeezed into the seat next to her. "Did you hear? Mrs. Freeman, the counselor, came right into first-period class and got Jessie. Do you think it has something to do with Susannah's murder?" Sybil's freckles stood out in stark relief against her pale face. "I mean, he's always been strange." She shivered. "Wouldn't it be awful if it turned out he was the one who murdered her?"

"Hey, you know what?" said Matt Goerring. "They came and got Nadia out of French class this morning. She looked real scared."

Melanie Russell looked around the table and grinned. "Maybe Jessie and Nadia were eloping, and they got caught."

"You read too many romances," said Matt.

Melanie flushed. "Well, *something* is going on."

"Cos must know what's going on," said Sybil. "I noticed he wasn't in history class. I thought that was funny, because he was here this morning. Where is he, Ari?"

"I'm not sure." Ari licked her dry lips.

"Whatever it is," breathed Melanie, "they must all three be in it together. They're probably . . . like . . . a gang!"

"Give me a break," said Matt. "Come on, Ari. Tell us what's up. You must have some clue."

"Jessie made some threats," she admitted reluctantly. "Cos thought somebody ought to be told." Suddenly she realized that Cos might not want everyone knowing that he had told on Jessie. "Don't tell anybody I said that!" she added hastily.

The other students at the table shook their heads soberly. "We won't say a word," someone said. Ari gazed around in despair. She knew the story would be all over the school before the end of the day. She might as well have announced it on the evening news.

Later that afternoon Ari realized that Nadia wasn't in chemistry class. Nadia and Jessie were probably both shut up with a counselor somewhere, spilling out their dark suspicions about vampires. Ari half expected someone to come jerk her out of class and demand that she come to the office and face their accusations. At least Paul was beyond their reach. She had never thought she would be grateful to her father for anything, but she was grateful for that.

As she gazed out the classroom window, she saw a sleek gray limousine drive onto the school grounds. *Jessie's father,* she decided. He had come to school to deal with the emergency.

Coming out of chemistry class, she almost ran into Cos.

"I've been waiting for you," he said.

She saw that his mouth was grimly set, an expression that was so unlike him that her heart fluttered in alarm.

"What happened?" she asked, gasping.

Cos looked around. Everyone in the hall seemed to be staring at them. "Let's get out of here," he said. "I can tell the whole school's talking already."

As Ari trotted beside Cos, holding his hand, she waited in agony for him to tell her what had happened.

"I feel sick to my stomach," he said tersely.

Outside, kids had spilled onto the lawns. Car pools were picking up riders. Ari was relieved she and Cos didn't run into Sybil, who would certainly have demanded to know what was going on.

"Let's go somewhere private," Ari suggested.

She and Cos found a table at a snack shop nearby. Cos chose a seat where he had a good view of the sidewalk. He shot nervous glances up and down the street.

"Where is Jessie?" Ari asked.

"I don't know. They wouldn't tell me anything," Cos said bitterly. "I'm just a kid."

"What happened when you went in to see the counselor?"

"I told her what Jessie said. I figured I'd better make it plain right from the start that he'd gone completely over the edge. So I gave it to her straight—all that junk about vampires, how he said he'd stalk and kill your entire family, the whole bit."

Ari noticed that Cos was unconsciously twisting a paper napkin into a corkscrew.

"Then Mrs. F. turned white as a sheet and said she was glad I had come to her." Cos snorted. "She didn't *look* very glad, I'll tell you. I could practically hear her knees knocking together. She jumped up and left me sitting there in her office for what seemed like forever. I tried to get up and go, but her secretary told me I had to wait." Cos passed a hand across his brow. "In comes the headmaster. I was in there the better part of the day, saying the same stuff over and over again. But that's not the worst of it. Jessie's dad came in, and I had to tell him, too."

Ari gulped. "That's horrible."

"He didn't say much. He just sat there looking like he'd been hit with a ten-ton truck. I swear, I felt awful, like it was *me* that was threatening to blow everybody's head off. Jessie's dad has always been real nice to me."

Ari grew cold when she realized how many people had been told that Paul was a vampire and that he had murdered Susannah. At first, of course, they wouldn't believe it. But the thought would return to them later when they lay in bed alone in the middle of the night. She knew how much closer and more real the supernatural seemed at night.

"I heard they pulled Jessie out of class," said Ari.

Cos heaved a sigh. "Yeah, but I never saw him, thank God. I was in a cold sweat, worrying that they were going to bring him in. I was afraid he'd look me right in the face and deny everything."

Suddenly it struck Ari how hard this must have been for Cos. He was the most sociable, lighthearted person she had ever met; that was what she loved about him. She had to admire that he had gathered his courage to tell on Jessie, even though she wished with all her heart he hadn't.

"I suppose they had him in some other room, keeping an eye on him," she suggested hesitantly. "Do you really think he would deny everything?"

"Sure!" snorted Cos. "Jess may be crazy, but he's no fool."

"I wonder what happened with Nadia," said Ari, thinking out loud.

"Nobody's worried about Nadia," Cos said, "because she's not going to shoot anybody. It's Jessie that's got the gun fixation. After all, it's not against the law to believe in vampires—it's just a little flaky."

They ordered cold drinks and fries. When the waiter left, Cos said gloomily, "I wonder what they'll do to poor old Jessie. He's going to hate my guts forever when he finds out what happened, that's for sure."

Just then Ari spotted Nadia and Amanda coming along the sidewalk. "Oh, no!" she cried. "Look!"

"Help," said Cos weakly.

To Ari's horror the girls pushed open the door of the snack shop and came in. Ari could hear their voices behind her.

"It'll do you good," Amanda was insisting. "No problem is so bad that hot chocolate won't help." Ari heard chairs scraping against the floor.

Cos's face was flushed. He was sitting stock-still as if he were a wild animal in sight of a predator. Ari sat in silence, praying that Nadia and Amanda would not notice them.

Nadia's intermittent sniffles were punctuated by Amanda's soothing tones. For the most part Ari couldn't make out what the two girls were saying, but occasionally a word or phrase would float her way.

"Maupin-Biggs . . . visitors . . ."

". . . *not* going to go to the funeral."

". . . mistake."

Ari heard a cup rattle on a saucer.

". . . true," Nadia said earnestly. "My grand-mother says . . . stakes in their hearts!"

"Let's get out of here," Cos muttered suddenly, grabbing the check.

Ari could feel the heat in her cheeks as they fled past the girls' table. She saw Cos shoot an uneasy smile at Nadia and Amanda.

Outside, the cold was a welcome relief. Cos wrapped his arm protectively around Ari, and the wind buffeted them as they crossed the street and walked up Massachusetts Avenue. Ari glanced up at Cos. He was pale from the cold.

"What's Maupin-Biggs?" she asked.

"Private psychiatric hospital," he said shortly.

"I guess that must be where Jessie is," she suggested.

"Sounds like it," he agreed.

"Well, here's my car," said Ari. Suddenly Cos pulled her close to him. His eyes softened as he looked into hers. "All day, I kept telling myself that I'd never forgive myself if Jessie did something to hurt you." He squeezed her until she was breathless.

"Are you going to visit him in the hospital?" she asked.

"No. How can I?" Cos was anguished. "When he finds out I've ratted on him, he'll be after me next."

As Ari got in the car, Cos placed one hand above the door and looked down at her with an expression that was hard to read. For a horrible moment Ari wondered if he suspected the truth.

"Oh, well, maybe they can fix him up at that place, huh?" he said at last.

"Yeah," whispered Ari.

As she drove off, she could see Cos in her rearview mirror, standing on the sidewalk. She felt a strange twist of her heart, as if she were leaving him for good.

The evil that poisoned her life and threatened to drag her into darkness was completely alien to Cos. He could never grasp the grim reality of the situation even when it stood clearly before him. The sight of his face in the mirror filled her with an aching loneliness.

CHAPTER
SEVEN

PAUL STEPPED INTO THE ELEGANT FOYER OF THE apartment. A spotlight sprang to life, illuminating an Oriental vase that stood on a low table.

"Is this place yours?" Paul asked, impressed.

"For now," said his father.

Paul saw that the key ring his father held in his gloved hand was monogrammed in gold with the initials B. H. "Who is B. H.?" asked Paul.

"A man of discriminating tastes," his father replied, "who won't be needing this apartment anymore."

"You mean he's dead?" asked Paul.

His father nodded. "When I realized that the cards in his wallet showed a good address, I decided to move in for a week or two, at least until someone discovers he's missing."

In the living room a pale-green rug had been rolled up, and a packing box full of china stood by a large bronze statue—a sleek modern sculpture of a headless striding man.

Richard smiled. "I'm packing some things up and sending them to a contact of mine in South America. The cash isn't exactly generous, but he fulfills my main requirement—no questions asked."

"You mean, you're stripping the apartment?" asked Paul, glancing around.

"You might put it that way. I prefer to think of it as redistributing the wealth."

Paul wasn't sure why he was shocked. He hadn't been surprised that his father had killed the man, after all. It seemed silly to get suddenly moralistic about stealing a few possessions from a dead man. He sat down on the low white couch. A handful of slips beside the lamp told him that his father had already sent many packages via Air Express to Argentina.

"I believe he owned an antique shop of some sort," said Richard, lazily trailing his finger along the gleaming surface of the bronze statue. "That is, if one can judge by the messages that keep coming in on his answering machine." The machine's light was blinking, and Richard switched it on.

A frightened woman's voice cried out of the small speaker. "Binkie! Please call me. I forgive you for standing me up, and I won't say another word about it—I promise. Just let me hear from you! I'm starting to worry!"

The next message was more impersonal.

"Hargrove, this is Taber. I've found a Tang

60

horse—bronze, eight inches tall, impeccable provenance. I thought it might interest you, but get back to me right away, because other parties are interested."

Richard switched off the machine.

"Isn't this kind of risky?" asked Paul. "What if somebody else has a key to the apartment and comes looking for him?"

"Don't worry," said Richard. "If that happens, I can handle it." He flipped a book open. "He had a fine collection of old books, but there isn't much market for that sort of thing in South America. Too bad that our friend Hargrove didn't go in for uncut gems. They're so easy to sell." Richard smiled wolfishly.

Paul looked around the apartment. A vast window showed the lights of Washington across the river. "Where do you sleep when you're here?" he asked.

"On the bed." His father smiled. "Hargrove had the place fitted with room-darkening shades. In a pinch I can bed down in a bathroom tub as long as there are no windows. For someone as tall as I am, it's uncomfortable—but it will do. Dragging a coffin around would only slow me down."

"I'll sleep in the tub," Paul said quickly. He was relieved there was no mention of his having to share his father's coffin. He still had vivid nightmares about when he had been forced to share with Aunt Gabrielle. Sometimes he woke up in a cold sweat feeling her sickly sweet breath in his nostrils and the clammy, cold flesh of her face pressed against his cheek.

A strain of music pierced the air. Paul turned around to see the digital numbers of a CD player glowing under the window. His father sat down beside him. "It's wonderful how many people have first-class sound systems these days," Richard purred.

Just then a high tone sounded insistently. Richard stiffened. "It's the doorbell. Ignore it."

A moment later Paul heard the key turn in the lock, and he looked at his father in alarm.

"Binkie?" a quavering voice called. A slender woman in jeans with her hair swept up on top of her head stepped into the living room. She stopped and gasped when she saw them.

"Binkie's been called away suddenly. He's on the trail of a Tang horse, I believe," said Richard smoothly. "But he kindly allowed us to stay on while he's away. I'm his friend Ricardo Montevideo, and this is my son."

Paul nodded at the woman, knowing as he stared at her pale, frightened face that he was looking at a woman who would soon die. She had seen them both at the apartment—now they had to kill her.

"Binkie didn't tell me he was expecting guests," she said, her voice unsteady. "I'm sorry for bothering you this late." She was agitated, and Paul could see the pulse at the base of her white neck. His mouth watered.

"Don't rush off," said Richard. "We were just

about to have a drink, and we're packing up this statue for Binkie. He has a buyer for it in South America."

"But Binkie said he'd never sell that!" She darted an alarmed look at the statue.

"Perhaps it's only a copy that he's selling," said Richard. "Let the lady have a look, Paul."

Paul met his father's eyes and knew Richard was inviting him to kill her. "I think it's the original," Paul said.

Suddenly he leapt on her and knocked her down. He heard her terrified gasp as he pressed her to the floor. Her eyes were bulging in fear, and she opened her mouth to scream. But before she could, he ripped her neck with his teeth, feeling the slight resistance of the trachea as his fangs tore through it. Air sighed out of her lungs and blew warm on Paul's damp face. He had almost severed her neck, and blood dripped from his eyebrows. Blinded by the blood, he thrust his tongue deep into the torn flesh. He heard a disgusting slurping sound and realized with detachment that it was he who was making it. He pulled away. Appalled at the raw look of the gaping flesh, he pressed both hands against it and felt, with relief, a surge of heat from his fingers. The bloody flesh took substance under his hands, and the gash closed.

He rocked back on his heels and surveyed the woman's body, his stomach heaving. Her mouth was slack and her face wore an astonished expression, as if she had been surprised by her own death. The touch of his vampire hands had made the woman's neck whole—but Paul could not erase from his own mind the memory of what had happened. He fell to his knees, overcome by nausea. Hearing his father's laughter behind him, he struggled to his feet and gasped for breath.

"You made a pretty mess of that one, didn't you?" said Richard. He leaned against the couch, one arm along its back, his legs crossed. Paul saw the glow of hot excitement in his father's eyes, the vicarious pleasure from the kill. He hated him for it. Before Paul could stop himself, he lunged. Richard moved aside so fast that Paul missed him and fell facefirst on the couch.

"Cut it out," snapped Richard. He stood next to the dead woman and nudged her body with his feet. "There's no need to get hysterical."

Paul buried his face in his hands. The couch was smeared with blood. "You were watching me," he said. "You made me nervous. That's why I messed up."

"It's over," said Richard curtly. "Forget it. Go wash your face." Richard glanced around the apartment. "I'll have to settle for what I've already gotten out of the place. We can't come back here."

Paul realized then that his father was putting on his gloves. A smile played on Richard's pale lips. "It's time for us to go for a walk," he whispered.

* * *

64

The storm moved in from the northeast with winds that bent the trees and sent shingles flying off rooftops. By midmorning the rain was relentless.

"What a depressing day for a funeral!" Cos muttered. He and Ari took seats near a window at the back of the crowded church. Ari could hear the rain against the dark glass.

In front of them a middle-aged woman blew her nose. The classmates around them were openly weeping. A pair of girls from Ari's chemistry class turned and stared at her for what seemed like an eternity. Ari felt her face grow hot. One girl whispered something to the other. Had Nadia been talking? Ari wondered. Was the vampire rumor spreading all over the school?

It looked bad that Paul hadn't come to the funeral—she was sure of that. Only yesterday she had been relieved that Paul was out of the way. But today she was painfully conscious that he should be here making a show, at least, looking brokenhearted.

The congregation rose, and Ari heard Cos's strong baritone voice beside her. She tried to concentrate on the music—anything to keep from thinking of Susannah's waxen body inside the coffin at the front of the church.

At last the service was over, and the choir moved down the aisle. Susannah's mother had to be escorted out, and her father looked thin and shaken, as if his knees were about to fold under him. Ari pitied them. How could Paul have been so wicked as to kill Susannah?

Outside the church cars lined up with their headlights on. Ari and Cos climbed into one. Then, slowly, they began following a long black hearse. Viewed through the streaming car windows, the city was blurred and indistinct. "They can't bury her on a day like this." Cos's voice was shaky. "The ground is pure mud." Ari grabbed his hand and held it tight.

At the graveyard, black umbrellas had mushroomed on the grass. Ari and Cos stood silently in the midst of the crowd, listening to the rain drum on their umbrella. Ari's skirt stuck to her legs. The priest raised his voice to be heard above the rain. "As soon as thou scatterest them, they are even as sheep and fade away suddenly like the grass."

Ari felt a sharp pain in her chest. Where was Paul?

Water oozed over Paul's sneakers as he bent to step into the culvert. "This way?" he asked doubtfully.

"Yes, follow me," his father called over his shoulder. "I want to show you something."

Paul could hear the frantic squeaks of rats as he followed his father into the darkness.

Soon it was so dark that only Paul's glowing eyes allowed him to see his father. The culvert smelled disgusting. The sticky bits of decayed vegetation reminded him of the slime at the bottom of a garbage disposal.

"I'm sick of this," he said. "I'm leaving." A flash of panic hit him as he realized he might have trouble finding his way out of the labyrinth of cement pipes.

"Wait! Don't go," cried Richard. "Here it is." Paul glanced ahead and saw that they had reached a junction of rough cement where the underground culverts joined the larger storm sewer system under the street. He turned and caught sight of a rat's garnet-red eyes gleaming at him in the dark. Paul met the stare. There was a small splash and the eyes vanished.

"See!" his father said. Richard reached up and ran his hand over a rough cement shelf about shoulder height.

Paul shrugged. "So what?"

"Don't you see?" Richard said. "It's always night down here. Rain or shine, it's the same. Here's a shelf you can sleep on. If you look around, you'll see there are all the rats you need for fresh blood. If you've pulled off some messy kill, and you're on the run, no one will ever think to look for you down here."

"Great," said Paul in a hollow voice. "Is this where you live?"

Richard's white fangs flashed. "No. It's for emergencies. Now that you've seen it, we can go."

Paul felt his way through the cement pipes. At last they came out into the slanting rain, and he exhaled with relief. He shook the rain out of his hair and shivered. More than anything he longed for a good hot shower.

He and his father walked silently down the street. "Hardly anybody is out on a day like this," Paul said, hoping his father would give up on the idea of making a kill.

A car whooshed past. Ahead of them stood an Italian restaurant, its furled umbrellas dripping in the rain.

"Can you spare a dollar, sir?" whined a thin voice.

Paul turned around. A toothless old woman, wrapped in shapeless clothes, squatted halfway under the steps of a nearby town house. A bulging plastic garbage bag sat beside her. Her hair, damp and dark with the rain, stuck to her pale skull. Paul reached in his pocket for a dollar. Just then he heard Richard's quick intake of breath, and before he could react, the old woman had completely disappeared under his father's broad cape. Paul blinked. It was like a magician's trick—now you see her, now you don't. His father's head jerked and the cape shuddered. Paul knew the old woman was dying under its black folds.

A crack of thunder set Paul's teeth on edge. He looked away. Suddenly his father was standing next to him, his eyes gleaming and his lips red with blood. Involuntarily Paul glanced at where the beggar had crouched. He saw only a heap of dirty clothes and a pale flash of flesh—a hand perhaps—in the shadows.

"Let's get out of here." Paul grabbed his father's arm.

Richard shook him off. "Calm down. Nobody's even going to notice she's gone." He licked the blood off his lips and straightened his collar. Paul saw that the rain running off his father's face was pink.

Paul walked in silence, listening to his father beside him whistling off-key. Richard's hard white flesh had taken on the faint glow of life.

"That was disgusting," Paul said suddenly. "A helpless old woman like that."

"Awfully high-and-mighty all of a sudden, aren't you?" Richard's eyes glowed at him. "Tell me, are your objections moral or aesthetic?"

Paul hunched his shoulders against the rain and said nothing.

"Too good to drink an old beggar's blood, are you?" Richard taunted him. "Maybe you're going to tell me you've never drunk a rat's blood?"

Paul felt himself grow hot with shame. "That's different."

Richard laughed. "It's always different when you're the one doing it. Ever notice that?"

Paul was astonished to find himself missing Aunt Gabrielle. Even her cold caresses seemed preferable to his father's company. Every night she went jogging and came back looking healthy and vibrant. Presumably she had fed, but he never saw her victims. *What the eye doesn't see, the heart doesn't grieve over,* thought Paul. Was he grieving over the old lady's death? he wondered. He supposed that he was. Her death didn't seem fair. She had so little—yet Richard had snatched even the small flicker of life she had.

"I ought to be getting back to Aunt Gabrielle's," Paul mumbled. "I can't afford to miss any more school."

"You don't need school." Richard's powerful arm engulfed him. "I can teach you a lot if you stay with me.

His father's touch sent a shock through him. Holding Paul tight, his father glanced up at a tall apartment building. "Here we are," Richard said. The peculiar satisfaction in his father's voice chilled Paul. He realized suddenly that he was powerless to escape.

CHAPTER
EIGHT

PAUL'S LEGS MOVED SEEMINGLY UNDER THEIR OWN will as his father guided him into the elevator. A faint, whining hum sounded in his ears, and his stomach felt queasy while the lit numbers next to the elevator door marked their ascent. Panic fluttered in his brain. He wanted to scream but couldn't. Every part of his body was numb.

The elevator doors opened into a hallway, and Richard slid a key into a nearby door. He pushed Paul into a dark apartment. The moment his father released him, Paul snapped out of his trance.

A light came on and he saw a reed-thin woman in a filmy white gown lying on a plush sofa. She raised herself up. Her eyes were startlingly violet and she wore a broad diamond choker.

"Hullo there," she whispered.

Paul stared at her serene white face. The

luminous eyes looked devoid of thought. "Who's this?" she asked, extending a hand that glittered with rings.

"This is my son, Paul," explained Richard. "Paul, this is Evangeline Wingate. Say hello." His father shoved him, and Paul found himself sitting beside the woman on the couch. She smelled vaguely lemon scented.

"Call me Evie." She patted Paul's cheek. "I'm sure we'll be great friends." She stood up, and Paul saw that her head looked rather too large for her bony, narrow body. Yet she was undeniably attractive. "You boys are wet. Wouldn't you like a shower and some dry clothes?"

"Yes, we would," said Richard. "You first, Paul."

Paul felt he had no choice but to go into the bathroom as he was directed and take a shower. He felt uneasy stripping in Evangeline's apartment, but at least the door was locked. Who was she? A vampire obviously. Her eyes gave her away. But what was her relationship to his father?

Paul turned the shower on very hot. His hard, pale skin did not feel heat the way his human flesh had, and it took much hotter water to relax the muscles that had tightened at the back of the neck. His overwhelming feeling was one of relief; at last he was out of reach of his father's paralyzing touch.

When Paul stepped out of the shower, the bathroom mirror was fogged with steam. He was startled to see unfamiliar jeans, a shirt, and a pair of briefs folded on top of the sink. He

tried the doorknob and saw that it was unlocked. Evangeline must have tiptoed in while he
was in the shower.

The clothes were loose on him. They probably belonged to Richard.

He tugged uncomfortably at the loose waist-
band of the jeans as he stepped out of the bathroom.

Music was playing somewhere. No one was
in the living room, so he peered into the next
room and saw that his father and Evie were
dancing cheek to cheek, swaying in time to the
music. The oak floor had been cleared for dancing, and the room's large window gave a blurred
view of the gray rain outside.

Evangeline and his father stopped and looked
at him.

"Your dad's clothes aren't a bad fit," said Evie.

"Now it's my turn in the shower," said
Richard. He pulled off his shirt to reveal powerful
broad shoulders and bony ribs. Stripped, he
looked like a starving boxer. He pushed past Paul.

Paul leaned dizzily against the door frame
and closed his eyes. He didn't want to be left
alone with Evangeline Wingate. He still felt peculiar. Whatever his father had done to him had
not worn off.

Evangeline drew close to him so that he
could feel her breath. She raised her brows at
him inquiringly. "Do you like to dance?" she
asked.

Paul shook his head.

She took his hand and led him back to the living room. "Then sit here next to me on the couch, and tell me all about yourself."

Paul couldn't think of a thing to say.

Suddenly she kissed him. He could feel her fingers brushing against his skin and realized she was unbuttoning his shirt.

Paul jerked away from her. "Stop that!" His one confused thought was that if his father came out and caught him kissing Evie, he would get killed.

"So you *can* talk," said Evie, looking pleased. She let her arm rest on the back of the couch.

Casting an anxious glance over his shoulder, Paul buttoned his shirt. He was hot with embarrassment. He could hear the shower running in the bathroom, and to his relief there was no sign of his father.

"Don't worry about Richard," said Evie. "He and I have an understanding. We both do whatever we want." Her lavender eyes darkened. "The only thing is, I don't want to do very much. It's funny how that is when nothing counts anymore. Have you ever heard of a game called Truth or Consequences?"

Paul shook his head.

"I think of it all the time, because once you become a vampire, there isn't any truth and there aren't any consequences, either." She smiled, and her eyes were empty of feeling. "I hear that Verena is the one who made you a vampire."

Paul felt anger flare dangerously inside him. He wanted to put his hands around Evie's jeweled dog collar and squeeze until she couldn't gasp out Verena's name.

"That was very naughty of her," Evie went on. "Richard was angry, because he thinks you were far too young." She tugged playfully on Paul's hair where it curled at the nape of his neck. "I personally like young vampires," she said. "They're so passionate and reckless." She giggled. "I'm placid to a fault myself, but they say opposites attract." To Paul's horror, she licked his neck.

"E-vie!" A roar came from the bathroom, and she jumped away from Paul nervously, folding her hands in her lap.

"So are you and Verena very special friends?" Her violet eyes opened wide. "I could have her over to visit if you like. She could even stay here. I have plenty of room."

The thought of coping with Verena and Evangeline together filled Paul with panic. "I hate Verena," he said. He racked his brain for a way to change the subject. "Where are you from?" he asked. "Where did you go to college? What was your major? Did you ever work?"

She laughed. "None of that matters now, Paul." Her finger traced a line on his arm. "Wouldn't you like to hear something really interesting, like how your father made me?"

"No!" he cried. "I wouldn't."

"It was wonderful," she said in her slow,

throaty voice. "I was married to a British diplomat in those days."

"That's interesting," said Paul desperately. "I used to think I might like to go in the foreign service."

"The parties were wonderful," she said. "Dancing, always dancing—and buckets of roses. I hear that these days the embassy puts on only dreary lunches where they try to get businessmen to invest in telecommunications." She made a face. "But in those days the diplomatic world had glamour. I met your father at an embassy party. I remember, at first I had the impression his name was Alexander Bodisco or something like that. It's never been exactly clear to me how he got an invitation."

Paul had a fair idea how. Presumably he had stripped it off of Alexander Bodisco's body.

"I really don't want to hear about this," Paul said desperately.

Evie placed a diamond-encrusted finger on his chest and laughed. Her fangs were small and pointy, like a bat's teeth. "Ah, but I want to tell you!" she said. "We had danced out into the garden—Richard is a beautiful dancer, and I adore dancing. I could hear the music from the ballroom, and light poured out the windows, making the camellias look like soft pale faces against the leaves. We danced close to the blossoms, and I almost swooned from their fragrance. 'You are so beautiful,' Richard whispered in my ear. 'And your voice is like honey. You intoxicate me. I want you to come away with me and live with me forever.'"

Evangeline's pale hands fingered her diamond collar uneasily. "Of course," her voice quavered, "I thought he had something quite different in mind."

Paul swallowed. "You didn't realize he was a vampire?"

She hesitated. "Not then."

"You should have run right back into the house," said Paul harshly. "You got what you deserved for fooling around. A married woman like you—you ought to be ashamed of yourself."

"My, what a Puritan you are!" She arched an eyebrow at him. "One almost wonders how Verena ever persuaded someone as upright and proper as you are to become a vampire!"

He heard the mocking irony in her voice. "I made one mistake," he mumbled. "That's all."

"One mistake is all it takes, isn't it?" she sighed. "Richard was so handsome, so forceful. I'm afraid the contrast with my husband was rather painful. I hadn't really planned to do anything but have a bit of fun. I'm not quite sure how I ended up taking that extra step." She laughed nervously. "I suppose I'm still trying to figure that one out. Maybe that's why I'm telling you this."

"You must have known he was a vampire!"

"Oh, yes. He admitted it. 'I must warn you I'm a vampire,' he said. 'You like that about me, don't you? Because you've got a little of the vampire in you.'" She gazed at Paul. "He knew by then, you see, that I didn't care."

77

Paul shivered. Had Verena sensed the vampire in him? Was that why she had attacked him?

"It hurt more than I thought it would," Evangeline added. Her voice was so distant that Paul wondered if she had forgotten he was there.

Paul had a sudden and vivid memory of the night Verena had dug her fangs into his flesh. "I don't want to hear this," he protested.

But Evie's slow, honey-thick voice went on as if he hadn't spoken. "'Don't you want to stay young and beautiful forever?' Richard asked me. Of course, I did. There's nothing wrong with that. Everyone wants to stay young and beautiful forever. It's not as if I did anything really wrong. I only wanted to look my best."

"Like Faust," said Paul.

Evie looked at him blankly. "I don't believe I know him."

"It's an old story," said Paul, "about a man who sold his soul to the devil."

Evangeline's pale face feigned polite interest. "How medieval sounding. I don't suppose they made that into a movie?"

"I don't think so."

"That explains it, then. I don't have much time for reading." She glanced in the direction of the bathroom. Paul could hear his father singing tunelessly in the shower. Evie went on. "I told him that of course I wanted to stay young and beautiful forever, and the next thing I knew I felt this blinding pain—I don't know how to describe it." Puzzled, she gazed at Paul. "It hurt beyond anything I had ever felt—and yet I wanted more of it. It seemed so important—everything else simply faded away as if it didn't exist. Then I got too weak to move, and all I knew was that Richard's heart was beating next to mine so loudly that I literally shook. It was like a drum in the midnight jungle—carrying some message that I had to know the meaning of but I couldn't quite grasp. Then everything went black." She touched her jeweled collar uneasily. "I know I passed out, though Richard says I didn't. He's a terrible liar. When I opened my eyes, I saw Richard's face over me, white as a magnolia blossom, and his fangs were dripping with my blood." She gulped. "It was a bad moment. I must confess, I used to be quite squeamish."

"Is something wrong with your neck?" Paul asked, a sick feeling seizing him. "Is that why you wear that necklace?"

Evie's eyes went blank. "He said he would fix it back as good as new," she said. "But something went wrong. Richard said it had never happened to him before. He blamed me. But how could it have been my fault?" She lowered her voice to a whisper. "In some light I can still see where his fangs went in. That's why I wear the necklace. Would you like to see?" She fumbled with the clasp of the necklace.

"No!" shouted Paul. "No, don't show me. Please don't."

Her eyes were blank. "It's not so bad. I'm sure a plastic surgeon could fix it—but I don't want to

79

go to a doctor. It might lead to a lot of questions."

There was a long silence, and Paul thought perhaps she had finished. The story of the hidden scar was the entire point of the story, it seemed. But then she began speaking again very quickly. "Of course, it doesn't matter really. Richard says I'm ridiculously self-conscious about it. And he's right. He's absolutely right."

"You don't have to tell me any more," muttered Paul.

"But I *want* to." Evie leaned very close to him and lowered her voice. "Richard bit his wrist savagely and pressed it against my mouth. Then he forced me to drink his blood."

Paul ran his finger along the inside of his collar. Suddenly it felt tight. "He couldn't force you to do that. It's not possible."

"Well, I had to, didn't I?" she said quickly. "It was either that or die. I suppose I hadn't really thought out the implications. One doesn't, does one? Not in the garden at night with a devastatingly attractive man. The moment, the beautiful moment, is all that matters. Only, I didn't expect it to be so . . . permanent."

Evie smoothed the white gown over her thighs. "I truly intended to go on as if nothing had happened, living with my husband and my three lovely children and going to parties. Oh, I do miss them. The children, the parties, everything," she said helplessly.

"You have three children?" Paul was surprised.

"Of course. But I haven't seen them in years. I never intended to leave my husband, but as it turned out, he simply couldn't accept that I had . . . changed."

Paul realized at once that it couldn't be helpful to a young diplomat's career to have his vampire wife luring her victims into the embassy garden.

"It was a shock for poor Derek! Appallingly so. I'm not sure what frightened him most—the scandal or the possibility that he was imagining the whole thing and that this was his first step toward insanity." She heaved a sigh. "He made a most handsome financial settlement for me, but unfortunately, in return I had to give up all visitation rights. I haven't seen the children since. We had a quiet divorce, and I moved in here with Richard." She glanced in the direction of the bathroom. "Well, not precisely *with* him, but he does keep most of his clothes here. I make sure they're kept cleaned and pressed. He's very particular."

Richard burst out of the bathroom, singing an operatic aria slightly off-key. He stopped singing suddenly when he saw Paul and Evie together on the couch. "Well, well, Evie. Having fun?"

She patted the sofa cushion beside her. "I'm telling Paul the boring story of my life. He wanted to know what I majored in in college."

Richard ran his fingers through his wet curls. "Oh? What did you major in?"

"History," said Evie in a flat voice. "Ancient history."

81

Richard glanced at Paul's bare feet. "Put on your shoes, Paul. We're going out."

"But you just got here!" protested Evie. "And it's still pouring rain outside."

Richard gazed out the window. "I always get restless on these rainy days," he said, straightening his collar. "There's no point in trying to sleep."

"Paul won't want to go out in all this," said Evie. "He can stay here with me until you come back."

Richard snorted. "Forget it, Evie. I'm not that stupid. Put these on, Paul." He tossed the wet sneakers to Paul. They smelled of the rotting vegetation in the culvert, and Paul gazed at them in dismay.

"And don't take all day." Richard's eyes narrowed. "I don't want to have to force you."

Paul hastily thrust his feet into the slimy sneakers and stood up.

"Find us an umbrella, Evie," said Richard. "And put Paul's wet clothes in a plastic bag or something so we can take them with us. We may not be coming back here." Richard strode over to the window. As Paul watched, his father's dark eyes glowed with an ominous red like the eyes of a rat. Richard was gazing down at the street with a look of naked hunger.

CHAPTER
NINE

JESSIE SAT ON HIS HOSPITAL BED, GAZING OUT THE window. The rain seemed to be letting up at last. Suddenly the door opened and a nurse poked her head in.

"You have a visitor," she announced. "Don't you want to come out and see her?"

"No. Send her in here," he said, frowning. He hated going out of his room to the open lounge area, where patients shuffled around in bedroom slippers and watched television.

The nurse shrugged. "Okay. But remember to leave the door open. Those are the rules."

A moment later Nadia tiptoed in. "Jessie?" Her dark eyes were wide.

"Calm down, Nadia." Jessie hastily tucked his shirttail into his jeans. "I haven't sprouted horns or anything, no matter what they told you."

"Oh, Jessie, this is terrible," she cried. "What are they doing to you here?"

"Nothing. I'm fine," he said shortly. "Sometimes they try to make me do crafts. This place is sort of like summer camp that way." He laughed bitterly. "And there's a lot of sitting in circles and talking, but that's about the worst of it. Besides, it doesn't matter what they do, because I'm getting out of here."

Nadia glanced over her shoulder at the half-open door. "But how? There are doctors and nurses everywhere, and all the doors are locked."

Jessie motioned to her for silence, then went into the bathroom and turned on the tap. He took Nadia's hand and led her to the open bathroom door.

"Wh-what are you doing?" she asked, obviously scared.

"Running water," he explained. "It helps drown out the sound of our voices in case the room is bugged."

Her eyes were huge. "You think your room is bugged?"

"Could be."

Nadia threw her arms around his neck. "Oh, Jessie, they seemed to know everything. The headmaster kept asking me if I'd talked to you about vampires or about killing people."

"What did you say?" Jessie asked her in a dangerous voice.

She pulled away from him. "I said, sure we had talked about stuff like that. But not *seri-*

84

ously. I said we were just kidding around."

"That was quick thinking," Jessie admitted grudgingly. "All things considered, you could have done worse. I wish I knew how they found out. It's like they tapped my phone. But it can't be that, because I'm always real careful what I say on the phone." He frowned.

"I just thought of something," said Nadia. "Do you think somebody could have heard what we were saying in the commons room yesterday?"

"Nobody was around," said Jessie, puzzled. "We were by ourselves."

"But somebody could have been hiding in there. What if somebody was following us, sneaking around and listening to what we were saying?"

He glanced at her. "You mean somebody like Ari!"

Nadia nodded energetically.

"You really hate her, don't you?" Jessie smiled thinly. "It couldn't be because you want to get Cos back, could it?"

"No!" cried Nadia. "It's not that. But, Jessie, she is so sneaky! She's always staring at me. It's like she's scared of me."

"It's me she should be scared of," said Jessie in a low voice. "I wish I could get out of this place."

"I thought you had a plan!"

"Oh, I know how to do it. I've been in this place before. The doctors want to keep me here because the patients are what pay for their boats and fancy cars. But if I act normal, pretty soon they'll run out of reasons they can give my father for keeping me."

"Coming here to visit is so creepy." Nadia shivered. "All of them treating you like a crazy person—I don't see how you stand it."

"It's simple. I pretend I'm somebody else." For a moment the only sound was of the rushing water in the bathroom sink. Jessie thought he'd better not let Nadia know that the person he pretended to be was Cos. When he was in those stupid therapy sessions, he'd always ask himself, *What would Cos say?* then he'd go with that. The hardest part was the inkblot test. No matter which way he turned the cards, he kept seeing eyes staring at him. Naturally he wouldn't admit that to the doctors. He told them he saw dancing bears and little rubber duckies.

"How can you pretend to be somebody else?" Nadia asked hesitantly.

"Easy. I keep telling myself that I like everybody and everybody likes me." He cracked his knuckles. "My line is that I may have been upset after Susannah was murdered, and maybe I said one or two things that were pretty wild, but I'm over it now."

"You're always so cool, Jessie." Nadia gazed up at him worshipfully. "You've got it all under control. When I found out they had put you in the hospital, I felt terrible, but now that I've talked to you, I feel much better."

"I'll get out of here." Jessie frowned. "The only trouble is that it's taking longer than I thought. Whenever I look at one of those doctors, it's like I see dollar signs in their beady little eyes." He gritted his teeth. "It makes it that much harder to tell myself that I like everybody, but I've got to. I have to get out of here fast. That's the only way I'll be able to fix Ari and Paul."

"I don't know, Jessie." Nadia's fingers worked nervously. "Maybe we ought to forget the whole thing. I had this talk with my parents, and the truth is—I think my imagination ran away with me, because there's no such thing as vampires."

Jessie laughed. "Come on, Nadia. Do you listen to everything your parents say?"

"N-no," Nadia said hesitantly. "But—"

"You saw the vampire at the school Halloween party, didn't you?"

Nadia gulped. "Yes. I did. His eyes glowed. It was horrible."

"And somebody or something drained all Susannah's blood out and killed her, didn't he?" Jessie went on insistently.

Nadia closed her eyes, pale now. "Yes," she whispered. "Amanda told me about how there was hardly any blood left in her."

"Something funny happened to me, too." Jessie's knees suddenly felt unsteady, and he had to put an arm out to brace himself against the wall. "It was that night I ran into Paul at the bar and his dad took me out back to show me a little pistol he had. I blanked out for a minute, and I figure he got some of my blood then. I felt weak for days." He took a deep breath. "Same thing happened to Sandy MacAdams. He spent the night at Paul's house, and the next thing we know, he's passed out and they're pumping pints and pints of blood into him at the hospital. Ari and Paul are vampires, all right. Everyone in the family is. All you've got to do is look at them." He shivered. "Those creepy eyes."

Nadia nodded. "You're right. Something really strange is going on."

"Damn straight," said Jessie. "I've got to get out of here so I can kill them before they get somebody else. My dad says he's sold all my guns, but I've got a few stashed away where nobody can find them." He glanced over his shoulder but saw only the gray light filtering into the bare room. "Nobody knows this, Nadia, but before they locked me up, I made some silver bullets." He glanced down out her grimly. "And I'm going to put every one of them into the hearts of those vampires."

Paul felt a sharp pain in his chest. He wasn't sure where the sensation came from—it was like a premonition of doom. He shivered as he walked quickly to keep pace with his father. The weather was raw with damp gusts of wind. The wet streets were deserted.

"Let's go back to Evie's," Paul pleaded. Surely his father had drunk his fill when he had killed the old lady. "How could you possibly still be hungry?"

"You don't understand," Richard said softly. "What I suffer from is hunger of the heart."

"I've been thinking." Paul cast an uneasy glance at his father. "I ought to be getting back to Aunt Gabrielle's. You said I could go back any time I wanted, you know. You promised."

Richard smiled. "Promises are for the future, and the future is an abstraction that does not exist."

"So you lied." Paul stopped walking abruptly.

"I do lie," said Richard tranquilly. "What matters is not truth, but beauty—untouched, undefiled, pure beauty."

Paul followed his father's gaze and was horrified to see that Richard was staring at a little girl sitting on the steps of a nearby house. Her face glowed with the dewy radiance of childhood. Her hair, shiny as glass, tumbled down the back of her red coat in loose curls. The front door of the house was open, and Paul could hear sounds of bustling activity within. Her mother must have gone inside for something. The little girl rocked her doll in her arms, singing to it.

Paul felt sick, cold fear in the pit of his stomach as he watched his father take off his glove. "No," Paul said. "I won't let you."

"And how will you stop me?" asked Richard softly. He brushed past Paul like the wind. Before Paul could blink, Richard was kneeling beside the child.

"Won't you show me your baby doll?" he asked.

The child shook her head and looked frightened.

Richard laid his bare hand over her mouth, covering her small nose as well, then pressed his lips to her neck. Paul was horrified to see the child's eyes widen and go blank. He was not even conscious of covering the distance, but suddenly his hands were around Richard's throat. Paul roughly pulled his father away from the little girl and threw him to the sidewalk. He was disgusted to see the glazed look of animal pleasure on Richard's face.

"Paige?" a frightened voice called. "Paige, where are you? Oh, no! My baby!"

Paul darted a glance quickly toward the steps. The child seemed to be okay. She was squirming in her mother's arms. Anxious to get away before the woman could get a good look at them, he grabbed Richard's arm, yanked him to his feet, and pushed him ahead.

"Keep walking if you know what's good for you," Paul said between clenched teeth. He was nauseated by the smirk on his father's face. Richard's lips were stained with the child's blood, and he smiled. "I'm going back to Aunt Gabrielle's house," Paul went on, unable to keep the disgust out of his voice. "You make me sick."

"Do you think I care?" His father's step was unsteady. "Go on back to Gabrielle. You're only nosing into what's none of your business, you goody-goody. You make a rotten vampire, you know that?"

Paul let go of his father's arm and walked away without looking back. He was cold to his bones. He shivered and hugged himself, scarcely knowing in which direction he was walking. The image of his father drunk on a child's blood horrified him. It must have been a small amount of blood—but maybe a child's blood was particularly potent. Not that he wanted to find out. It was disgusting! Even knowing that he was related to Richard made him feel unclean. He needed to get home and find Ari. He was sure that would make him feel better.

Some vague homing instinct took Paul in the direction of Georgetown. He glanced up and saw the gold dome of Riggs National Bank, a single bright spot against the gray sky. Walking just ahead of him was a slender young woman. Wisps of her short, dark hair curled charmingly around her ears. He found his pulse racing but was unsure why until she suddenly turned and looked at him.

"Sophie!" he cried. She quickened her pace, but he ran after her and caught up. "Come on," he pleaded. "Give me a break. It's so great to see you! I've missed you."

She touched her hand to her cheek, and Paul was overcome with remorse. He shouldn't have hit her, but she had made him mad, acting as if he belonged to Verena.

"I'm so sorry," Paul said. "Give me another chance. Please, Sophie! I want to see you again."

"I'll think about it," said Sophie. Her ice-blue eyes gleamed with an unearthly light that thrilled him.

"Where are you going now?" Paul asked.

She shook the rain out of her hair. "I'm only out walking. On these dark, rainy days I can't sleep."

Paul gazed at her high cheekbones, slightly flared nostrils, and sensitive pale lips. *Delicate and flowerlike,* he thought, his heart turning over. "Can't I go along with you?"

"No." Her blue eyes were like stones.

Paul felt anger flare inside him with a force that frightened him. Swallowing hard, he struggled to control it. *I am not like my father,* he told himself, clenching his fists. *I can control myself.* He sensed this was a test. Somehow he had to prove to Sophie that he could rein in his temper. "Can I see you again, at least?" he asked, his voice shaking with the force of emotion.

She smiled a little. "If you want to."

"I want to." His eyes met hers, and he could feel his gaze grow searingly hot. "I want to in a big way," he said.

"We could go to Lou's some night," she said. "It's a club where we could dance."

They settled on a time, and feeling as elated as if he had won the lottery, Paul headed toward home. He would be seeing her again! Sophie— even her name was like a song.

When he reached Aunt Gabrielle's mansion, he smiled. After what he had seen on the visit to his father, the gloomy old house on N Street looked wonderful. Never would he have dreamed that he would be so glad to get back.

CHAPTER
TEN

A KEY TURNED IN THE LOCK, AND THE FRONT DOOR flew open. "I'm home!" Paul yelled.

Ari was so surprised at the sight of her twin that she fell against the gong at the end of the hall. It made a dull sound that echoed down the long hallway. "You missed Susannah's funeral," she cried.

"I'm sorry." Paul rubbed his nose self-consciously. "I'm going to do better, Ari—I promise."

"What's wrong?" Ari couldn't decipher his expression, but she was worried. He had said he would be away for several days, and he was back in fewer than forty-eight hours. What had happened?

"I can't live with our dad," Paul said. "He's . . . well, I can't live with him, that's all. I've got to make my life here. I see that now."

"Paul!" Aunt Gabrielle came running down the stairs. She threw out her arms to him.

"Hi."

They embraced and Aunt Gabrielle stared at him, her eyes brimming with tears. "You're looking awfully well," she said.

Too well, thought Ari, noticing that Paul's face had the telltale flush of a recent feeding.

Aunt Gabrielle wiped tears from her glistening eyes. "I'm sorry to be bawling. I really am so happy to see you. But I've just had the most dreadful news. Poor Wiley Hoban—they've fished his body out of the canal! You remember him. He made those wonderful Halloween costumes for you and Ari. It almost makes me wonder if he was leading a secret life. Otherwise why would anyone murder a harmless old man?"

Ari glanced at Paul and was disturbed to see that his eyes looked blank, as if shutters had been pulled down behind them. *Poor Mr. Hoban,* she thought. Did he have something Paul wanted? Or was it only that Paul was thirsty for blood?

"Well, enough of that," said Aunt Gabrielle, blowing her nose. "Paul, dear, I've talked to a lawyer about your legal situation. I've made a few notes about what he said, and I need to go over them with you."

Ari didn't want to hear about what Aunt Gabrielle euphemistically called Paul's "legal situation." She ran upstairs to her room at once and closed the door. She wondered if rainy days were always going to unnerve her. It was day-time, and vampires should have been asleep in their coffins. But when the gray skies made a kind of uneasy twilight, they stirred and walked the streets. It was horrible!

Ari absently arranged the chess pieces on the chessboard. Instantly one of the pawns toppled over. Holding her breath, she straightened it. It fell over again. Her heart began pounding. She wondered suddenly what Rab was doing. She shook her head. The less she thought of him, the better. Why was some odd undeniable link pulling them toward each other?

There was a knock at her door, and she jerked her hand away from the fallen pawn. "Come in," she called.

Paul came in and glanced at the chessboard. His eyes seemed to soften. "Where'd you find that?" he asked.

"It was in the basement with the other things from our old house. Something is wrong with one of the pawns, though. It keeps falling over."

Paul picked up the queen. "Remember how we used to play chess on the front porch in the summertime?" A faraway look was in his eyes. "We've shared a lot, haven't we? Remember how Mom said we used to speak our own private language?"

"Glub-glib," said Ari promptly.

Paul laughed. "Jeez, it's been so long since I've laughed."

"Why can't you live with Dad, Paul?" Ari asked. "Tell me the truth."

He hesitated. "He's bad, Ari. I mean, evil. I don't want to go down the road he's gone down. I've got to put my life back together and make the best of the way things are here."

But it's too late for that, thought Ari.

"I can do it," Paul said, giving her a quick glance. "I know you think I can't, but I can. I've bought some strong sunblock, so I can go out in daytime just like anybody else. I'm going to go back to school and finish my education."

He caught a glimpse of himself in Ari's mirror and walked toward it, smiling. "Not bad," he said, tucking a strand of hair behind his ear. "I don't know why I never noticed before that I'm the type girls go for."

Suddenly Ari was frightened. "Please stay away from Sybil!" she pleaded. "Promise me you will."

He flashed her a smile. "Hey, don't worry. I'm not that hard up. I've got a hot date this weekend."

Ari closed her eyes. "You aren't going to kill somebody else, are you?"

"I made one mistake with Susannah," he snapped. "It looks like you're going to hold it against me the rest of my life." Checking his image in the mirror, he pulled a comb from his jeans pocket and ran it through his hair.

"What about Mr. Hoban?" asked Ari.

Paul wheeled around suddenly. "How did

you know about him?" he demanded.

"I didn't," said Ari bleakly. "Until now."

Paul sat down on the chest at the foot of the bed, and the pawn fell over. He put it upright.

"It keeps falling over. I think that means somebody is going to die," said Ari.

"Somebody is always going to die," said Paul impatiently. "That doesn't mean I'm going to kill them. Lay off me, will you?"

"What happened with Mr. Hoban?" asked Ari. "Did you want his blood? Was that all it was?" She knew her voice was shrill.

"I don't need much blood to keep going," said Paul angrily. "The man insulted me. I asked him to help me out, and he said I wasn't normal! I guess I just lost it for a minute." Paul's eyes grew dark and lusterless. "He ought not to have said that. He could have helped me out—if he'd wanted." He walked over to the window and looked outside, gripping the sill tightly with his white hands. "I've got to learn to get ahold of my temper. I can do it, too. I'm going to school tomorrow and behave just like anybody else."

When she thought of Paul mingling with the other kids at school, Ari's heart sank. "Jessie knows you're a vampire, Paul. Cos and I were sitting in the commons room, and we heard him and Nadia talking about it. He said he was going to lie in wait for you and me and Aunt Gabrielle. He says he wants to wipe out all the whole nest of vampires at once."

"I can handle him." Paul glanced at Ari. "But

97

you better be careful. It might be a good idea for you to leave the house by the back way from now on. He might try to shoot you or something. You know what a nut he is."

"People know!" she cried. "It's getting around school! Don't you see? Kids are going to be looking at you, wondering if you look . . . strange."

"I look fine," said Paul, suddenly laughing. "I look great. Listen, Ari, nobody's going to listen to Jessie. It's a known fact that he's certifiable. I just wish Cos hadn't heard what Jessie said about me." He frowned. "It's embarrassing."

"Cos is not the problem, Paul," Ari said wearily. "Cos would never do anything to harm me. The problem is Jessie! They aren't going to keep him locked up forever."

"He's locked up?" A slow smile spread over Paul's face as he turned to face his twin. "In jail?"

"A psychiatric hospital," admitted Ari reluctantly.

"Even better." Paul rubbed his hands together. "I told you he was crazy, Ari. Be cool. This is going to be a piece of cake. You worry too much, you know that?"

The next morning Ari and Paul drove to school together. As they drew close to St. Anselm's, they passed Sybil's car pool, and Sybil waved to them cheerfully out the car window. It seemed impossible to Ari that Sybil didn't notice how Paul had changed. Ari herself could think of nothing else—his pale, hard-looking skin, his strange, glimmering eyes.

When they got out of the car at school, Ari saw that the sky was heavily overcast with a layer of clouds that looked like smoke. Since the weather was raw and unpleasant, few kids were lingering outside. Ari rushed into the building and immediately looked around for Cos. He was nowhere in sight.

Behind her she heard her twin saying sadly, "I went out and put some flowers on her grave."

Her head turned sharply. He was standing near the door with a group of kids gathered around him.

"It seemed better to go out there by myself." Paul sounded choked up. "I couldn't face the funeral. But the graveyard was worse. I can't stand to think she's under the ground there—her beautiful golden hair."

Ari was stupefied. Paul sounded so convincing! For a brief instant she found herself wondering if it was possible he had gone to the graveyard and put flowers on Susannah's muddy grave the way he'd said. Then she remembered that he must have had no idea where the grave was. She pressed through the crowed, desperate to get away from the sound of his voice.

"Hey—hold on." Cos turned a corner and caught her by the arm. He smiled. "I see Paul is back. Is he feeling better?"

Ari nodded. "He's sad about Susannah, of course."

"Poor guy."

"What do you hear about Jessie?" Ari glanced up at him anxiously.

"Not much," said Cos. "He's still in the hospital. I haven't had the nerve to go see him."

"You think they might keep him locked up for good?"

Cos shook his head. "Nobody gets locked up for good these days. But his dad sold his gun collection. That's the important thing. No matter how crazy Jessie gets, I can't see him trying to kill anybody with his bare hands."

"He wouldn't get far trying to kill Paul with his bare hands." Ari shivered suddenly.

"I've never understood this gun fetish of Jessie's." Cos frowned. "It's weird to feel like somebody's mind is so dark you can't make out how it works."

"Yes," said Ari, her voice subdued. "I know exactly what you mean."

"Let's quit talking about this," said Cos. "It's getting me down."

They had reached the commons room, and Cos hesitated at the archway a moment. Then he pulled Ari into the room. "You know how they say when you fall off a horse you ought to get right back on?" His eyes gleamed with mischief.

In spite of herself, Ari laughed as they fell together into the big leather chair. Cos kissed her and she snuggled close to him, forgetting everything else for a moment.

"You!" screeched a shrill voice.

Ari felt blood rush to her face. Nadia! Ari clutched Cos's shoulder tightly. If she hadn't been sitting on his lap, she was sure she would have passed out from shock.

"Hi, Nadia," said Cos weakly.

"You were spying on us!" cried Nadia. "I knew it! I told Jessie you were sneaking around after us. How could you do this to me, Cos? How can you be on *her* side? You used to love *me*." She burst into tears suddenly, then turned and fled. Ari heard her quick footsteps running away down the hallway.

Cos was pale. "Jeez," he muttered. "What have I done to deserve this? I swear, I feel like changing my name and leaving the country!"

Ari touched his cheek. "She has to see that we didn't come here to spy on her. We only came here to have a little quiet time together."

"I don't feel very quiet right now," Cos snapped. "Get up."

Ari leapt to her feet. They walked to class together in silence. As they made their way through the crowded halls, Ari had the feeling people were staring at them. "If it's not all over school already that I'm the one that blew the whistle on Jessie, it will be now," said Cos bitterly. "And when he gets out, he's going to be really mad." He shrugged in an unconvincing effort to look unconcerned. "Not that it's any big deal."

Ari felt sick that she had brought so much trouble to Cos. *He would be better off without me,* she thought dismally.

To Ari's surprise the week that followed went by quickly and quietly.

No major dramas erupted. Nadia didn't shriek accusations at her. Instead she seemed to be avoiding both Ari and Cos. It seemed impossible that Paul could go to school and behave like an ordinary student, but he did. By mutual agreement Ari and Cos gave up on making out in the big leather chair in the commons room.

Friday Ari spotted Conner O'Hara coming out of the boys' bathroom. He leaned against the wall and doubled over. To her alarm she saw that he was deathly pale. While Ari stared in horror, Paul came out the bathroom door, his face glistening with freshly applied sunblock.

"You okay, Conner?" he asked. "Need some help getting to class?"

"Paul!" Ari's hand flew to her mouth.

He met her gaze. "I think Conner may have a touch of flu," he said.

Ari was sure Paul had been sucking Conner's blood. His eyes gleamed like liquid fire, and his face looked hot. But she couldn't bring herself to say anything else to him about it. Conner's eyes had a glazed expression, but it wasn't as if he were unconscious. He would hear anything she said to Paul. After looking helplessly at the two of them for a moment, she hurried off, her emotions in turmoil.

Ari couldn't concentrate the rest of the day. Her mind kept floating back to Conner. Had she done the right thing? She knew she would never forgive herself if Conner died. But was it possible that she was overreacting? After all, maybe he really did have the flu.

Finally, when the twins were driving home that afternoon, Ari couldn't contain herself any longer. "Paul! What did you do to Conner?"

"He was coming down with something, that's all," said Paul. "Don't look at me like that."

"You're lying!" she cried.

"Oh, stop it, Ari!" snapped Paul. "For your information people have more blood than they need. What I took didn't hurt Conner—he's going to be fine. You saw him standing up, didn't you? How bad off could he be?"

Ari stared out the car window, feeling cold inside.

"I quit the cross-country team this afternoon," Paul went on. "I told Coach that I need to concentrate on my schoolwork. He was disappointed, of course, but he said my studies had to come first and that I was making the right decision. The thing is, I can't risk running. These days it's hard for me to keep from going too fast. I don't get winded and tired the way I used to, and sooner or later somebody might notice that I don't sweat." He touched her arm. "I just wanted you to know that I'm making an effort, Ari. I'm not taking any stupid chances."

Ari didn't know what to say. She and Paul used to be able to read each other's minds. Now she wasn't sure she understood him at all. How could he kid himself that it was okay to prey on Conner? Of course, she knew Aunt Gabrielle had to drink her victims' blood, but usually Ari didn't have to see what happened. She didn't have to see them looking like Conner—white and staggering from weakness.

"It's going okay so far," Paul said, gingerly fingering his chin. "My skin feels funny, but I don't think much sun has gotten to me. I keep running in the bathroom and putting on more of that sunblock. It's pretty obvious I'm still upset about Susannah, so nobody even mentions her to me. People are very respectful of my grief." He smiled into the rearview mirror. "Just the same, I don't think I'll spread it around that I'm getting back to having a normal social life. In fact, tonight I've got a hot date."

"Paul," cried Ari, "please don't kill someone else!"

Paul laughed. "Don't worry, Ari. She's a vampire."

CHAPTER
ELEVEN

THE CLUB WAS DARK, ITS WALLS PAINTED WITH FLU-orescent murals of snakes coiling up purple mushrooms and poisonous-looking flowers. At a group of tables in one corner some thin, pale couples were drinking Bloody Marys. A woman in a silver dress shimmied alone in the center of the dance floor. Her long blond hair almost completely covered her face as she jerked her head in time to the music. Paul could see her eyes glowing under the veil of hair.

A young man with a scraggly beard sat on the floor with a drum between his legs. The drum frame was covered in purple snakeskin. Nearby some skinny men with guitars strummed a tune.

Paul knew he was at a vampire club. A faint, warm stink of blood hung in the air, and Paul could hear a high, thin sound in his brain—the song of vampires gathering together.

Then he spotted Sophie at a table in a dark corner. He felt almost weak with relief that she had shown up.

"This place has almost *too* much atmosphere," he observed when he reached her.

Sophie smiled. "Want to dance?"

Paul pulled her to her feet and drew her close. He had never cared for dancing before, but with Sophie it was different. When her body was close to his, he felt a pulse of excitement beating in his ears. "Are you still writing poetry?" he asked, gazing down at her heart-shaped face.

She nodded. "I want to make something beautiful, even if it's something small like a poem."

"I love that about you," he said.

She looked down, and he could see the pale-blue blood vessels in her eyelids. Her blood would make the world sing. Even thinking of it made his stomach quiver with excitement. He felt sick with desire. "Sophie," he said thickly, "do you think you could ever feel really close to me?"

"Maybe," she whispered.

As they danced, the scene around them grew dim and insubstantial, as if it were the moving and shifting reflection on a river's surface. The river of illusion was eternal and would run forever, Paul thought. The strange drum would play, the woman in the silver dress would shimmy, and the glasses of red blood would refill themselves endlessly.

As he guided Sophie into a turn, Paul suddenly saw that the woman in the silver dress was on the floor.

"Don't look!" said Sophie.

A man was holding the woman down, and her blond hair was splayed out on the cement. In spite of himself, Paul focused on the man's mouth. His lips, fringed by a disgusting brown beard, were pressed tightly against the woman's neck. Suddenly the man's lips drew back, and Paul saw that his yellow fangs had sunk deep into the woman's flesh. The silver dress jerked spasmodically.

"Is she dead?" Paul gulped.

"How can she be dead?" asked Sophie. "She's a vampire." She stopped dancing. "Why don't you buy me a drink?"

They took seats at the small table, and Paul signaled a waiter to bring drinks. They tasted terrible—homogenized and stale. Paul remembered being told that outdated blood-bank blood was sold at these places.

He could not stop himself from stealing glances at the couple writhing on the floor, though he noticed that everyone else in the room carefully avoided looking at them.

The music had grown wilder now, and a couple of men began doing a Russian dance in the middle of the dance floor, their arms crossed over their chests. Paul was surprised to see that he recognized one of them, a muscular vampire in a black T-shirt. A tiny gold stud glittered on one nostril.

"That's Dubay," confirmed Sophie, following his gaze. "He's the one who made Verena."

She gave Paul a sidelong glance, and he realized she was testing him again. He could feel rage swelling inside him like a balloon, but he gulped it down. "I hope he doesn't come over here to talk to us," he said. "I don't like him."

Sophie looked at Dubay through half-opened eyes. "Don't you think he's kind of cute?"

"Sophie!" Paul cried.

She stirred her drink with her straw. "He's not really my type, though," she went on.

Paul laid his fingers on the pulsing blue vein that ran down the side of her neck. "Why don't we find some place really dark where we can be alone?" he said, thinking how nice it would be to press his lips against that blue vein.

Sophie bent her head to the side, baring the curve of her neck. "What's wrong with right here?" she asked.

Paul opened his mouth with a sharp intake of his breath and bit. His teeth were immobilized by the firm flesh, and he rasped his tongue against her skin. Instinctively he bit harder so that her flesh pressed against the roof of his mouth. He heard her moan, and at last he felt her blood spurt inside his mouth.

Gradually he lost consciousness of his body until he was aware only of the surging rhythm of her heart and his. Suddenly a bolt of pleasure threatened to split him in two. They fell and started rolling together on the floor. He felt a dull pain in his neck as Sophie's hair tickled his ear. He wrapped an arm around her, squeezing her close. More pain, deeper pain—he wanted it. The lights in the club pulsed in time with his heart, and he felt weak from her scent. The dark room was expanding as if it were a membrane growing thinner and paler. It stretched to the breaking point.

"Oh!" he cried, blinded suddenly by a shower of multicolored stars.

"Paul?" Sophie's breath tickled his ear, and he laughed. "Are you all right?"

Her heart-shaped face came into focus then, a pale shifting image as if she were made of fumes. "I'm great," he sighed. "Great."

She opened her fingers wide like a starfish and covered his face. "Happy?" she asked.

"That was so strange," he murmured.

"Vampire love," Sophie said. "It does seem kind of sick, doesn't it? All that pain." She shivered. "I remember I was totally disgusted at first."

Paul felt a sharp pang of jealousy. "You've done it with somebody else?"

"Dubay," she said, smiling.

Paul sank back onto the floor. The pain of knowing Sophie had been with Dubay felt sharper than when her fangs had sunk into his flesh. It suddenly hit him that he couldn't trust Sophie any more than she could trust him. "It's okay about Dubay," he said weakly. "I don't care a bit. It doesn't matter."

"Liar." She smiled. She was leaning on one elbow, lying stretched out on the cement beside him. She rolled over on her back, and he saw her fangs when she yawned. "Can I trust you, Paul?" she asked softly. "I mean, really, really trust you."

He smiled slowly. "Yeah," he lied. "Sure you can."

As Ari gazed up at the night sky, a star fell in a blurred arc and was gone. "I've never seen a shooting star before," she said.

Cos squeezed her hand. "I'm really glad you decided to come, Ari. You can see why I didn't want to come by myself. Everybody's paired off like it was Noah's Ark."

Ari smiled in the darkness. The air was so cold, it hurt when she breathed, but she didn't care. For the moment she was free from her vampire family, hidden by the thick woods. She had left only a vague note on the refrigerator, telling Aunt Gabrielle she was going camping.

Giggles and the sound of thrashing branches marked the approach of the other kids. "It's cold!" complained Melanie Russell.

"Nah," said Conner robustly. "It's not so bad."

Ari had had mixed feelings when she'd found out that the cabin where they were camping belonged to Paul's victim, Conner. She couldn't stop herself from looking at Conner anxiously, checking to see if he was still pale. But as far as she could tell, he was fine.

Amanda was there too, with Blake Robinson, a tall, brutal-looking boy whose gruff manner frightened Ari.

The three couples stood together at the edge of the river. Ari's heels sunk down in the soft earth as she gazed up at the sky.

"Have you seen anything?" asked Amanda.

"Only one shooting star so far," said Cos.

"Some people have all the luck," said Amanda. "I'm getting a crick in my neck, and we still haven't seen a thing."

Ari wondered how much Nadia had told her friend Amanda about her notion that Susannah had been killed by a vampire.

Conner shivered. "Maybe it is cold after all," he said. "I guess we'd better get back inside."

No one argued with him. The stars twinkled in the sky overhead with an icy brilliance. They headed back along the narrow path to the cabin, their breath making clouds of white in the air.

When they pushed open the cabin door, they could smell dinner cooking on the coals of the fireplace. Ari pulled her sleeping-bag roll close to the fire and perched on it, reveling in the heat. Cos sat next to her, and the others gathered around the fire in a semicircle.

"I hear Jessie got out of the hospital today," Conner said. Ari stiffened.

"That's right," said Amanda. "I told Nadia I'd ask you if they could come, but she thought

Jessie'd better take it easy for a while and not try to do anything like camping at first."

Conner's relief was obvious. "Yeah, you're right. He should take it easy." He glanced uneasily at Amanda. "I hope he's okay now," he said. "Somebody told me he thought vampires were after him. That is pretty crazy, you have to admit."

Ari looked away, afraid her face would betray her.

"Jessie's fine now," said Amanda airily. "Maybe he was a little upset after Susannah was murdered. We all were. But the whole thing's been blown out of proportion."

Ari glanced around the circle and noticed that Cos looked miserably self-conscious. He was obviously still racked with guilt about having turned Jessie in. Several times already this week he had explained to Ari that turning Jessie in was the only possible thing he could have done—probably more to convince himself than her.

"I smell something burning," said Melanie.

Conner pulled the aluminum packets off of the coals so that they left a trail of smeared ashes on the hearth. He slit open a packet, and a cloud of steam rose. "It's only a little bit burned around the edges," he assured them.

They had gone fishing on the river that afternoon, and the fish, with lemon juice and butter, was the main course. They also had ears of corn glistening with browned butter. Ari watched the other kids balancing plastic plates on their laps. Their faces were pink from the heat of the fire.

"Hasn't it ever hit somebody that maybe there *is* such a thing as vampires?" asked Blake.

Ari looked at him in alarm.

Melanie giggled. "Cool. Every camping trip I've ever been on somebody's started telling ghost stories."

"I think you're supposed to wait until the fire's burned out and everybody's about to go to sleep, though." Conner was talking with his mouth full.

"No, wait!" Blake held up a huge hand. "This isn't a ghost story. This really happened to my dad when he was posted in Greece. Honest."

Melanie stared at him. "*Vampires* really happened?"

"Not exactly," he said.

Ari distrusted Blake instinctively. Despite his huge bulk, his eyes were small and close together. His nose looked as if it had been broken and badly reset. He lowered his voice. "This really happened to my dad when he was posted in Greece when he was younger. He had read about oracles, and he went to this cave where people say the oracles used to live back in the old days. I guess he was trying to get a feel for the oracle thing. He wanted to soak up the atmosphere."

Blake paused, his eyes watching the crackling fire. "Dad had to bend down low to get in the cave," he went on, "but as soon as he got inside,

113

he could straighten up. Then he could see there was some kind of red light ahead, so he started inching up toward it. Something smelled funny, and he began to wonder if he ought to go back in case it was poisonous fumes. Then he turned a corner, and this shriveled-up woman was sitting there on a rock, mostly in the dark, but a red beam of light came down from the roof of the cave and sort of spotlighted her. She was wearing a tattered old sweater, tennis shoes, and thick socks, and her hair was matted. My dad was wondering what's going on, because it was a really weird place to find an old lady. Water was sort of trickling over the rocks, the place was cold, and it smelled bad. But my dad said hello very politely in Greek. Then the old lady's eyes rolled up so all he could see were the whites of her eyes."

"She was the oracle!" breathed Melanie.

Conner looked interested. "I read a book like that one time. They got that red effect by putting a pane of red glass over a light hole."

"Do you guys want to hear the rest of the story or not?" demanded Blake. He shot a hostile glance around the circle.

Everyone stopped talking. The coals popped and flames rose suddenly.

"Then the old lady jumped up from the rock and screamed, 'You've come for the gold! But it's too late. They've stolen the gold—those who drink blood have stolen it!' My dad said she sounded hoarse, like something was stuck in her

114

throat. 'Their hearts will burn like coals,' she said, 'and their blood and bones will shrivel into ashes. Curses on them and their children. They will regret the day they stole my gold.'"

The room fell silent for a minute.

"When did this happen?" asked Cos.

"In the sixties sometime."

Cos grinned. "I wonder what your dad was smoking."

Blake wadded up some tin foil and threw it at him as the others laughed.

But Ari was not laughing. She remembered that Paul had found a hoard of gold hidden in a secret cabinet behind Aunt Gabrielle's fireplace. He had said the treasure looked very old. Ari froze with fear. Was the gold cursed?

CHAPTER
TWELVE

"PAUL! PAUL!" ARI RAN IN THE FRONT DOOR AND tossed her sleeping bag on the marble floor. Suddenly she stopped. Paul was asleep in his coffin. How could she have forgotten?

The big doors to the living room had been pushed back. Ari peered into the dim room. On the mantel was a golden French clock, decorated with blue and gold signs of the zodiac. Heavy velvet draperies stifled all sounds from outside. Except for the quiet ticking of the clock, the room was eerily silent.

Ari wished Paul were awake. She knew that he would not be afraid to go in the room. Holding her breath, she crept in and went over to the fireplace where the vampire gold was hidden. Its mantel had been carved into the shape of a pretty woman's face wreathed with curly leaves. Ari let her fingers slide over the surface of the cold marble and pushed at it with the heel of her hand. When she heard a click, she stopped breathing. The face pivoted easily in its stone socket to reveal the face's other side—a carving of a macabre skull, its jaw held on by shreds of rotting flesh. Even though she had seen it before, Ari could not stop herself from recoiling instinctively.

Paul had told her he believed the twirling face on the mantel was a kind of combination lock. Gritting her teeth, Ari twirled the double-sided face around a couple of times, first one way, then the other. If it were a combination lock, she realized, the number of possible ways to turn it must be nearly infinite. But suddenly she felt the mantel move. She gulped and stared in astonishment as a dark crack opened along the side and top of the fireplace. It had opened like a door! Ari grasped the edge of the marble and pulled. The marble slab swung open slowly.

She could see then that behind the fireplace a chest of drawers had been shaped to fit the wall. Ari opened a drawer and saw the glint of gold. She slammed it shut and placed a hand over her chest, trying to catch her breath. Her heart was beating so violently, it felt as if it might leap out of her body. Moving quickly, she opened one drawer after another. Most of them were filled with gold coins. She picked up small jeweled bottles and unscrewed their tops. Their sweet scent made her dizzy, and she screwed them closed again. Finally she opened a long shallow drawer in the center. There, lying on black cloth, were three thin, flat masks of gold. This was the oracle's gold—she was sure of it! The masks were exactly like pictures she had seen of gold stolen from the graves of ancient Greek kings. Surrounding them were gold disks that looked as if they had once been part of a necklace.

Suddenly Ari heard footsteps. She hastily closed the drawers and glanced over her shoulder, bumping her hip against the mantel to push it back into place. To her relief she heard it click shut. It had closed behind her as easily as if it were a large and heavy door.

Carmel, Aunt Gabrielle's housekeeper, stood before her at the door to the living room. Her dark hair was wrapped in a long braid around her head, and she was carrying a black umbrella.

Ari struggled to smile. How much had the housekeeper seen or guessed? Carmel began talking in rapid-fire Spanish. Ari wished she had taken Spanish instead of French in school. She never had the slightest idea what Carmel was saying.

Saturday was the housekeeper's day off. She shouldn't have been coming in today. *"Sábado?"* Ari inquired tentatively, drawing on her tiny stock of Spanish.

Carmel waved the closed umbrella, and Ari understood her suddenly. The housekeeper had left her umbrella and had come back for it. An ordinary thing. And yet dangerous. Ari knew she should have been more careful. She should at least have made sure the doors to the living room were closed before she'd tried to open the fireplace.

"Okay," said Ari weakly. "That's good. *Bueno.*"

She walked with the housekeeper to the narrow back hallway, glancing in passing at the servants' dark staircase, which her father had often used for slipping upstairs unnoticed. Still weak from the shock of finding the gold, she stood at the tradesman's entrance and waved to Carmel as she left. Overhead the skies threatened rain.

A few hours later, after dark, Paul and Aunt Gabrielle appeared. "I got your note," said Aunt Gabrielle. "How was your camping trip, dear?"

"Okay," said Ari shortly.

"I guess Cos was there, huh?" said Paul with a sour glance at Ari.

"A bunch of us went."

"You sure spend a lot of time with that guy," he said.

Ari heard an unmistakable note of envy in her twin's voice. "It's not like you're sitting at home being bored," she retorted. "What about that vampire girlfriend of yours?"

Paul's eyes flashed fire, but he didn't answer.

Aunt Gabrielle pottered around in the kitchen. Ari watched her aunt slide a casserole into the microwave. "What's the point of all this cooking?" Ari said. "I'm the only one of us who eats." She ran her fingers impatiently through her dark curls. "It's so stupid for us to sit down to a big meal every night when we're only going to throw most of it into the garbage."

"There's a certain discipline to living as a human being," Aunt Gabrielle said serenely. "I can't let myself slip up when it comes to these small details."

"Or she might end up like Dad," Paul added, with a sidelong look at his aunt. "That's what she's thinking."

Aunt Gabrielle pursed her lips in reproof but didn't answer. She went into the dining room, set the table, and turned on the crystal candelabra. Its glow was reflected by the glittering panes of the French doors. Ari followed her aunt into the dining room, feeling as if her nerves were jumping around inside her skin. She couldn't stop thinking about the vampire gold. It seemed odd that the fireplace had unlocked its secret on her very first try. The mantel had opened for Paul the first time he had tried it, too, and not long after that, Paul had become a vampire. It was almost as if the mantel were a living thing that had its own reasons for luring both twins to get a glimpse of the gold. Had it been a fatal mistake for her to open the fireplace? Perhaps the gold had the power to pull them both into the darkness of the vampire life. She gazed out the French doors at the dark garden behind the house and shuddered.

"I think that casserole must be ready," said Aunt Gabrielle. "Let's sit down."

Ari and Paul took their seats. Aunt Gabrielle brought in the casserole and poured some wine. "It's so nice for me to have a real family life at last." She sat down across from them. "That's what I've always wanted, you know." She dabbed at her eyes with her napkin. "Always. Ever since the night I became a vampire, I've regretted that I didn't have a family of my own."

Ari wanted to respect her aunt's fantasy that they were an ordinary, happy family. But the absurd pretense made her want to scream. She gripped her fork tightly. "Blake Robinson told an interesting story last night," she said. Glancing first at Paul, then at Aunt Gabrielle, she recounted the story of the old lady and the curse she had put on the gold. When she finished, neither of them spoke.

"So, what do you think?" Ari prodded. "Isn't that strange?"

"Very," agreed Aunt Gabrielle dryly. "I used to know Ben Robinson years ago in school, and I had no idea he was interested in Greek history."

"I mean about the curse!" cried Ari. "Don't you see that if anybody had that gold, what they should do is get rid of it!"

Paul laughed. "You aren't getting superstitious, are you?" He examined his glassy nails. "Blake probably made the whole thing up."

Ari bit back a sharp retort. She had to watch what she said. Aunt Gabrielle didn't know that Paul had discovered the gold, and Ari knew Paul didn't want her to. It was clear that Aunt

Gabrielle was not prepared to share the gold's secret.

Ari took a deep breath. "What I don't understand," she said, choosing her words carefully, "is why anybody would be stupid enough to steal the gold in the first place. It's not as if it could be sold on the open market. One look and anybody would know right away that it was stolen. If it's the gold of the ancient Greek kings, I suppose it belongs to the Greek government."

"I bet you could sell it in South America," Paul put in, "with no questions asked."

Aunt Gabrielle gave him a sharp look. Ari's heart skipped a beat. Had she inadvertently given her twin away?

"I'm only guessing," Paul added hastily. "I've never tried to do anything like that myself."

Aunt Gabrielle twirled her wine in her glass and studied the light reflected in it. "Maybe the gold has some sort of ritual power. Some kind of magical importance." Aunt Gabrielle lifted her eyes to meet Ari's. "Just suppose that the gold had some great power for good or ill. Then it might be worth someone's while to steal it."

Ari wanted to shake them both and scream, *Can't you see this gold could destroy us all?* Why did they refuse to listen to her? Did Paul really hope to sell the gold in South America? Did Aunt Gabrielle actually know that it possessed special powers? Ari couldn't be sure. But one thing was obvious—neither Paul nor Aunt

Gabrielle had any intention of getting rid of the cursed gold.

After dinner Paul and Aunt Gabrielle went upstairs and came down dressed for jogging. Paul tied the sleeves of his sweatshirt around his waist. "I may have dropped cross-country at school," he said, "but I want to keep running to stay in shape."

Pink shiny tights cloaked Aunt Gabrielle's thin legs, and her dark hair was tucked up into a baseball cap. She smiled the enigmatic half-smile that didn't show her fangs. "Aerobic exercise is marvelous," she said.

Lies, Ari thought. *Nothing but lies.* Knowing they would jog through the dark streets looking for victims, she watched them leave the house. The idea didn't even shock her anymore. She felt only a dull sense of disgust.

Once they were gone, she went into the living room and stared at the fireplace. Should she try to take the stolen gold herself and return it to its rightful owners? Could she be certain this was the gold Blake had been talking about? And what would happen if she mailed pounds and pounds of stolen gold to Greece? The packages might get inspected at customs! Of course, she wouldn't put a return address on it—but did the government have ways of tracing these things?

Ari turned away from the mantel. It was stupid to worry about returning the gold when she didn't know who the rightful owners were. She wasn't even sure she could make the fireplace's combination work again. And she didn't know for certain that getting rid of the gold would remove the oracle's curse. Worst of all, if the gold came up missing, Paul and Aunt Gabrielle would know she had taken it.

The doorbell rang and Ari nearly jumped out of her skin. Sybil stood on the door stoop, her cheeks flaming from the cold. Behind her, tall and solemn, was Rab, a burgundy muffler wrapped around his neck. "Rab and I are going out for hot chocolate, and we thought you and Paul might like to come along." Sybil gazed down at her feet self-consciously, her red hair shining under the porch light.

"Paul's out jogging with Aunt Gabrielle," said Ari. "But I'll come."

Ari's one thought was to get out of the house fast before either Rab or Sybil noticed anything was wrong. She was suddenly afraid of the strange fireplace in the living room. What if it opened unexpectedly? The very thought made cold sweat break out on her forehead.

Ari kept silent as Rab drove to a doughnut shop. They went in, got hot chocolate at the counter, took it to a booth, and sat down. "I guess you heard Jessie's out of the hospital," said Sybil, lifting the whipped cream off her steaming chocolate. "What I hear is that his breakdown wasn't serious. It was just that he was upset about Susannah. Of course, we are all upset, but I guess it's tougher for somebody like Jessie. It probably brought back memories of that time he was kidnapped in South America. That's my theory, anyway. You know, like the flashbacks Vietnam veterans have? Don't you think it's funny that the people who talk the toughest sometimes fall apart the fastest? I mean Jessie talks super-tough, but you really can't tell what's going on inside a person at all."

"No," said Ari. "You can't." She took a hasty sip and burned her mouth.

Rab looked at her. "I keep hoping I'll get to meet your brother, Ari."

"He keeps awfully busy," said Ari. She dreaded the day that Rab's sharp eyes would bore into Paul. At least the kids at school did not seem to have noticed that anything was wrong with him. She had worried that they would at first; then she had realized that most of them were amazingly self-involved. They were always gazing in the bathroom mirrors, obsessing about their bad hair or a zit. Maybe that was why they hadn't noticed Paul had changed. As for Sybil, she turned red and stuttered every time he got near. No chance she would take an objective look. But Rab was different. He had a way of looking at people that took in everything, then seemed to see right through to the other side. It was bad enough that he had met her father.

As they ate, Rab told them about his applications to law school. He spoke absently, and Ari had no idea what he was really thinking. *You really can't tell what's going on inside a person at all*, she thought.

Sybil stirred her hot chocolate, rattling her spoon against the cup. "I hope you get into a law school that isn't too far away. It's been great having you come home more often." Her eyes met Ari's in a brief, meaningful glance. Ari knew that Sybil thought Rab was coming home more often because he was falling for Ari. Ari hoped she was wrong.

"I ought to be getting home," she said.

"What's the rush?" asked Rab.

"I've got homework," she lied.

Rab stared at her. "Okay," he said reluctantly.

She was relieved when at last they reached Aunt Gabrielle's house.

"I'll walk you up to the door," said Rab, getting out of the car before Ari had a chance to object.

Just then, to her horror, Paul and Aunt Gabrielle came jogging up. Sybil leapt out of the car. "Paul!" she squealed in delight.

Paul and Aunt Gabrielle looked as nearly human as was possible. The healthy look of their flesh told Ari they had drunk their fill tonight. She hated herself when she realized she was past caring about their victims. All she wanted was for Rab not to have any inkling of the truth. "Aunt Gabrielle," Ari said, "you remember Sybil's brother, Rab. Rab, this is my brother, Paul."

Rab and Paul shook hands. "You look a lot like your father," said Rab, gazing at Paul.

Paul shot Ari a startled glance.

126

"Rab gave our father a ride a couple of weeks ago when his car broke down outside Charlottesville," she explained.

Aunt Gabrielle smiled complacently. "All the men in my family are amazingly good-looking, if I do say so myself."

"And the ladies, too," Rab said with a slight bow, but Ari could see curiosity glittering in his eyes.

"So gallant," cooed Aunt Gabrielle. "Rab, won't you and Sybil—"

Ari cringed. She knew her aunt was about to ask them into the house, but her sentence smoothly changed course, "—give us a call the next time you're in town," she went on, glancing at Ari. "And perhaps we can get together."

"It's awfully cold," said Ari, stamping her feet. "We'd better go inside."

Paul's white teeth showed in a half-smile that concealed his fangs. "See ya!"

Ari sighed with relief when they got inside away from the Barrons' curious eyes. She leaned against the front door, breathing hard, and watched Aunt Gabrielle shrug off her pink jacket. Shadowed by her baseball cap, Aunt Gabri's violet eyes glowed in the dark like radioactive jewels. How could Rab and Sybil not notice that Paul and Aunt Gabrielle were vampires?

"Rab doesn't look much like Sybil." Paul hopped on one foot as he pulled off a shoe. "Jeez, he's tall. Sybil's a shrimp, but Rab's taller than I am."

127

"He's awfully smart, too," said Ari ominously. "I hope he didn't notice that anything was wrong."

Paul laughed. "What's to notice?" He clasped his bony hands together and stretched. "We look great!"

Ari stared at him in disbelief. How could Paul deceive himself that way? She wondered in what other ways he was refusing to see the truth. "Paul, Jessie is out of the hospital. You're going to have to be very careful. You know that, don't you?"

"Good grief, Ari. Lighten up! I'm not afraid of Jessie."

Ari couldn't take any more. She turned suddenly and ran upstairs. Behind her, she could hear Aunt Gabrielle asking in a querulous voice, "Who is this Jessie? And why was he in the hospital?"

CHAPTER
THIRTEEN

"SURE, I BELIEVE IN THE SUPERNATURAL. IN FACT, I have a little personal experience along that line. One time I shook hands with a zombie," said a familiar voice.

Ari whirled around and saw Blake leaning against a classroom wall and talking loudly. Amanda and Nadia were in front of him, looking completely captivated.

"The only thing you can do with a zombie or somebody like that is to drive a stake through their hearts. Then they can die in peace."

Ari squeezed her eyes shut and ran down the hall in a panic. Suddenly she collided with Jessie.

He grabbed her arms. His icy blue eyes bore into hers. "Watch where you're going," he said, his teeth clenched. "But I guess you don't worry about getting hurt, do you? Vampires like you."

"I don't know what you're talking about," she

gasped. She felt his fingers bite into her flesh as he held her tight. "Let me go!" she cried. "You're hurting me!"

He let go suddenly, and his expression went blank. Involuntarily Ari glanced over her shoulder and saw that Cos was coming toward them. He reached them the next second and slapped Jessie on the back. "Jess, man, it's great to see you. How's it going?"

"Great," Jessie said in a flat voice. "I'm great." He turned abruptly and walked away.

"He's mad at me," said Cos, glancing over his shoulder uneasily. "He knows I'm the one who ratted on him." Ari heard the sharp intake of Cos's breath. "He doesn't look so good, does he?"

"I'm scared of him," Ari whispered. "He grabbed hold of me so hard, he hurt me."

Cos looked troubled as he put his arm around her. "I don't know what to think. He looks the same on the outside, but his eyes are empty. Did you notice that? Things are weird around here lately. People are acting strange, and it's not just Jessie."

"He's the worst of them," said Ari.

"I guess, but he's not the only one. It's like some mass hysteria. Do you remember when we learned about the Salem witch trials in history class? People start talking about witches, satanic cults, vampires. Next thing you know, everybody's believing it. I heard Blake down the hall, telling Amanda and Nadia that he knew a

130

zombie *personally*. Beats me how you could know a zombie personally. I mean, aren't they dead?"

Cos's eyes were sparkling, but Ari couldn't manage a smile. "I don't know. But I don't like it," she said.

Cos shrugged. "I don't like it either. But you've got to take things the way you find them. It wouldn't be the first time I'd put up with stuff I didn't like."

It suddenly struck Ari that Cos's common-sense attitude was completely and utterly insane.

Jessie went into his bedroom and glanced at the empty gun rack, his face expressionless. He unlocked a chest at the foot of the bed and gazed down into it, feeling desolation cut into his heart. It was true, then. His father had sold all his guns. At the bottom of the chest lay a few lonely ammunition clips. It had taken him years to build up his collection, and now it was gone. And he knew whose fault it was—those vampires. It was their plot against him. He knew Cos had ratted on him, but he didn't blame him for it. Cos was under Ari's vampire spell. She and Paul were the cause of all his trouble.

He opened his closet and removed a pair of smelly sneakers. With a fingernail, he pried at the knothole in the floorboard where the shoes had been. He lifted the board up. He felt giddy with relief when he saw the gleam of dark metal.

131

His father hadn't found these guns, at least. Jessie took the three pistols out of the hidden cavity and spread them out on the floor. He caressed them lovingly. The big semiautomatic was the best of the lot, but it took a clip. It wouldn't work with his handmade silver bullets, so that meant he would have to depend on his reliable old revolver. That seemed fitting anyway. The old-fashioned pistol was the simple, basic gear favored by survivalists.

"Jessie?" Nadia's anxious voice came from outside his bedroom door.

Jessie shoved the gun back into his hiding place and replaced the board. He tossed the old shoes on top of it and jumped up.

"What are you doing here, Nadia?" he demanded, throwing open his bedroom door. "You know I'm going to be too busy tonight to go out."

She sat down on his bed, her eyes large and frightened. "I want to go with you."

"You can't do that. This is no job for a girl."

"I can be your lookout," she pleaded. "Please don't leave me sitting around worrying all night, Jessie. Please!"

It suddenly struck Jessie that there might be certain advantages to having Nadia along. The chief one was that his parents liked Nadia. It was easy to see why—you only had to look at her to see how harmless and fearful she was. Since Jessie had gotten out of the hospital, his mother had been watching his every move. But Jessie was sure she would think that he couldn't get into any trouble if Nadia was with him.

"Okay," he said. "You can come. But you've got to do everything I say. And I mean everything. I don't want you getting hurt."

She smiled. "Thank you, Jessie. Do I get to take a gun, too?"

"No! You don't know anything about guns. You'd only end up shooting yourself in the foot."

"That's not true," said Nadia indignantly. "I took target shooting at camp. I'm actually a pretty good shot."

He looked at her with new respect. "No kidding?"

"I won the junior marksman's prize," she said with simple pride.

"It might not be bad to have a second gun along," he admitted. "The thing is, I'm not sure how fast these vampires can move. It's not like they're human. We can't be sure what we're up against."

"I'm not worried," sighed Nadia. "I used to be scared of vampires, but with you along, I know I'll be safe."

Jessie parked two blocks away from the Montclairs' house. He and Nadia got out and moved quickly toward the mansion. He wasn't worried about being seen. If anybody spotted them, their story was that they were out for an evening walk. But as the tall mansion came into view, Jessie held his breath. On the face of it the Montclair place didn't seem that different from any of the other neatly kept town houses. The lacquered black door gleamed in the lamplight. A pot of dark pansies stood beside it. But Jessie noticed that the windows of the living room had been hung with heavy velvet curtains that were unlike the curtains on the other houses. And the middle upstairs window had been completely blocked up. Whoever lived in this house was very fond of privacy—or darkness.

"This is the place," Jessie said to Nadia. "Follow me."

A tall wooden gate opened onto the narrow path that ran between the house and its garage. Jessie was relieved to find that it wasn't locked and that the gate's hinges were well oiled so that it slid open noiselessly when he pushed it. Nadia followed close on his heels. Jessie left the gate open a crack. "We'd better keep quiet," he murmured. "We don't want them to hear us. We can see from here when they come out, and then we can follow them."

Nadia's white teeth flashed in the darkness as she smiled. "Okay," she said.

Jessie had begun to wonder if it had been smart to bring Nadia along. He had thought having her along would make it easier to get out of the house without a lot of questions from his mother, but it turned out his mother had gone out for groceries before Nadia had even arrived. She still hadn't returned when they'd left. Now, as he set out following the vampires, Nadia was going to be a problem.

"I want you to stay here and wait for me," Jessie insisted. "Two people trailing them are going to be easier to spot than one."

"No way. If they turn around and see us, all you have to do is kiss me, and it won't look a bit like we're following them."

Jessie grinned. *She might have a point,* he realized.

"I'm going with you," she insisted.

"Paul, I want to see you." Sophie's voice was husky on the phone and it sent chills up Paul's spine.

"Fine," he said quickly. "Where?" Sophie was like an addiction. He never had enough of her, and the sound of her voice sent a pulse racing in his temples until his head hurt. "Soon," he said urgently.

"At Lou's," she said. "As soon as I can get there."

After he hung up, Paul smoothed his hair back and licked his lips. He checked his image in the mirror. Why did Sophie never let him pick her up at her place? he wondered. He had no idea where she lived. What was she hiding? he kept asking himself. He pushed the unwelcome thought away. Forget that. The important thing was that he would be seeing her soon!

His eyes felt painfully hot, and he gasped with emotion as he ran downstairs. Sophie! He had to have her. It was a passion such as he'd never felt before—not a human emotion, but the feeling of the sort a lion must have. He remembered that female lions had long gory gashes on their backs, put there by their mates. That was the way it was with him—he wanted to tear into Sophie's flesh until her thin blood choked him with its force. He burst out into the night.

Paul had an odd, uneasy feeling as he passed the gate beside the house. He looked at it sharply but saw nothing. Still, as he walked toward Wisconsin Avenue, the uncomfortable feeling continued—a sensation of danger. Quickly he glanced over his shoulder and froze. Two dark figures were walking behind him, and he saw the reflected gleam of pale hair. Jessie! The small girl with him must be Nadia.

Paul quickened his step and turned, heading in the direction of the canal. He was so angry, he could feel blood vessels expanding uncomfortably in his head. This nasty complication meant he was going to be late. Sophie might even think he had stood her up. He couldn't risk leading Jessie to the club where he was supposed to meet Sophie. He could lose them, but as the blood pounded painfully in his temples, he knew he didn't want to lose them—he wanted to punish them for ruining his evening.

He could hear the rushing of water in the canal lock. Automatically he glanced over at the row houses that lined the canal. Wiley Hoban's shop used to be lit at night, but tonight that shop was dark like the others, its curtain drawn tight for good. Paul ran down the steps to the canal path. Hidden by the darkness, he darted quickly along the water and up the next set of steps. He doubled back silently and stood by a tree, watching Nadia and Jessie arguing.

"I won't let you go down there," Nadia whispered. "It's dark. He could be hiding anywhere."

"This is exactly why I didn't want to bring you along," Jessie whispered angrily. "Let go of me. I'm going after him."

"Looking for me?" Paul asked lazily.

Jessie wheeled around and made a jerking movement with his hand. Paul felt a sting on his chest and looked down to see a neat black hole in his windbreaker. He laughed, but it was angry laughter. He felt his eyes burning with rage. "No good, Jessie. You can't get rid of me that way, you know." A bullet whistled past his ear. He advanced slowly on Jessie, smiling as the other boy reached in his pocket and took out a sharp wooden stick. Paul laughed. Jessie actually believed in that stuff about hammering a stake through a vampire's heart! It was comical.

Jessie pressed the point of the stick against Paul's chest and shrieked as he pushed with both hands, trying to press the point in with the heels of his hands. Paul's windbreaker ripped as the stake slid down his hard flesh. Furious, Paul grabbed hold of Jessie and shook him like a terrier shaking a rat.

"Don't hurt him!" Nadia screamed in Paul's

ear. Ignoring her, Paul clamped his fangs tightly onto Jessie's neck.

"No!" Nadia was tugging at his jacket. Jessie had gone limp in his grasp and was pale. Paul turned his head and smiled at Nadia, his lips dripping with blood. He showed his teeth and saw her face freeze with horror. Unconsciously his hands loosened on Jessie, and he let the other boy's body slip from his grasp. He scarcely noticed as Jessie fell to the pavement. Nadia backed away from him, but a few steps took her to the brink of the drop to the canal path. She could back up no farther. She held a small pistol in her hand, but it shook, and she seemed to have forgotten how to use it. Paul reached for her, folding his arms around her like a lover. He heard the gun clink against the bricks as it fell from her hand.

"Please don't hurt me!" she pleaded. Her dark eyes were wide with terror, and Paul felt excitement stir deep in the pit of his stomach. She was warm with quick pulsing blood, and she smelled of fear. He put his hand over her mouth and smiled as she struggled. Stopping her mouth with one hand and holding the other behind her neck, he pushed her back, half-lifting her with no more effort than if she were a kitten.

He pushed her down on a green bench under a nearby tree. The humor of killing her on the bench struck him, and he grinned suddenly. Anyone who happened to catch a glimpse of them would think they were kissing, but this

138

kiss was the kiss of death. He loved the feel of her clean dark hair as he buried his hand in it, wrapping it around his fingers like a horse's mane. He jerked her head back sharply. Her neck strained, the sinewy muscles showing tight under the skin. The big veins in her neck bulged in terror as he bent his head and bared his fangs. He bit deep at the white flesh, and her blood gushed into his throat. A steady pulse coursed warmly though his body. He felt her desperate squirming stop, but her heart was strong, and blood jetted into his throat. He wanted to savor the moment, but he had become uneasily aware that Jessie had moved.

Just then he heard a sound like a car backfiring and felt stinging in his back. Annoyed, he turned around to look at Jessie, who stood quivering and white as a ghost in the darkness. The pistol shook in his hand.

Paul grinned. "You're next, Jessie. It's going to be a pleasure to drink your blood."

The gun fell to the pavement with a clatter, and to Paul's surprise Jessie bolted. Paul saw him running away, disappearing into the darkness quickly. He licked the salty blood off his lips and sat down on the bench next to Nadia, putting his arm around her still, warm body almost affectionately. She was dead now; her eyes stared blankly ahead and her struggles had stopped. He felt warm to his toes and content. If he ran after Jessie and caught him, that would make him even later going to meet Sophie. Paul closed

139

Nadia's startled-looking eyes with his forefinger—already they had lost their luster.

Jessie was no danger to him, he decided, getting up. Jessie might start babbling about vampires, but nobody was going to believe the word of someone who was fresh out of a psychiatric hospital. Right now Paul was more interested in seeing Sophie. Something glittering caught his eye, and he bent to pick it up. A silver bullet! Paul laughed, tucking it in his pocket.

Jessie sat leaning against a dark building, cold sweat running down his face. Even when he replayed the awful scene in his mind, he couldn't be quite sure what had happened. Paul had come at him, and Jessie knew he had fired again and again, several times at point-blank range. His ears still rang from the sound of the shots. He couldn't possibly have missed Paul, but even the silver bullets hadn't killed him. The sharpened stake he had brought along just in case had slipped off Paul's chest as if the flesh were steel. It had been worse than a nightmare. Somehow Paul had grabbed him, his eyes glowing in the darkness like coals, and everything had gone black.

When he had come to, he'd seen Paul bending over Nadia's limp body.

Nadia! He had to go back there. If only he could erase the memory of how he had run away! But it had been something he couldn't control, a wildfire of fear. Now he had to make himself go back. He couldn't be a coward. Steadying himself with one hand against the building, he stood up. His knees were shaking and he felt weak all over, but he forced himself to stagger down the sidewalk. Dark shadows reached for him like black hands. He shivered. Only intense effort kept him moving toward the sound of the water rushing in the lock.

At last he saw the large tree that cast a skeletal shadow along the canal. On the bench under it, a small dark figure sat, her head bent. Nadia! A surge of panic sent him running over to her, the weakness in his legs forgotten.

"Nadia," he breathed, grabbing her shoulders. Her head rolled over. "Nadia!" He was sobbing now. "Talk to me. Don't die. You can't be dead!" He gripped her wrist, but he felt no pulse. It dawned on him that she felt cool, and he realized her mouth had fallen open. She was dead!

He turned away suddenly and vomited. His stomach squeezing painfully, he leaned his forehead against the rough bark of the tree and wiped his mouth with his hand. He could hear her voice echoing in his brain: *I'm not worried. I used to be scared of vampires, but with you along, I know I'll be safe.* She had trusted him to keep her safe, and he had let her be killed!

He knew he couldn't go to the police. He shot a frightened glance at Nadia's body. They would suspect him! Fresh out of a psychiatric hospital, boyfriend of the dead girl—he was the perfect suspect. With tears stinging his eyes, Jessie backed away from the body.

Paul felt disoriented when he first stepped into the darkness of Lou's club. Some major redecorating had occurred since his last visit. The dark room was filled with wispy, drifting clouds—produced by bins of dry ice, he supposed. Beams of colored light moved in the darkness, turning the clouds red and blue. When the colored beams fell on the ceiling, cut-out star shapes glittered brightly.

At last he saw Sophie at a table in the corner. When he reached her, she was tapping on the table impatiently with a pink enameled fingernail. Clouds billowed around her heart-shaped face in the shifting light. "You took your time getting here," she said.

"I couldn't help it. Somebody was following me." Paul sat down across from her at the tiny table and nudged her foot with his shoe. "I didn't want to lead them here to you." He glanced around. "Lou's redecorated." Paul smiled at her. "Nice."

"You stink of blood," said Sophie. "I guess that's why you look so pleased with yourself."

Paul laughed. "So what?" He slipped his jacket off and put his hand through a long tear in the material. "Some guy from school came at me with a gun." He shrugged. "He tried it all— silver bullets, sharpened stake."

"The superstitious type," observed Sophie.

"Is it his blood that's warming you so nicely?"

"Not his. His girlfriend's," said Paul.

Sophie stiffened.

"I didn't make her into one of us or anything." Paul smiled. "You're still number one with me, Sophie."

Sophie turned her head away, and Paul's gaze was drawn to the delicious curve of her bare white shoulder and neck. "I don't care what you do," she said. "Not a bit."

Paul leapt across the table then and knocked her to the floor. He had pulled the tablecloth down under him, but it didn't seem to matter. Sophie was giggling as he sank his teeth into the china-white flesh of her neck. He felt as if he were floating, and in a flash—like the sudden hot stroke of lightning—he understood what his father had said about the different kinds of hunger. He was sated with Nadia's blood—but still he wanted Sophie.

Paul bit so viciously that he felt the strain in his jaw. He sank his teeth deep into her neck, then shook his head, tearing at the hard flesh. At last a stream of thin, intoxicating vampire blood shot against the roof of his mouth. He was wild with excitement. A split second later he released her and was staggered by deep pain. A black shade fell over his eyes, and he moaned with pain deeper and more terrible than he had felt before.

"More," he muttered incoherently. "I can take it." The burning pain split him in two. At last, when neither of them could stand any more, they lay together on the cold cement floor, exhausted.

Paul stared at the glittering star shapes on the ceiling, breathing hard. He realized suddenly that he would hate for Ari to find out how he and Sophie spent their time together. It was disgusting. But he admitted to himself that there was nothing like the thrill of it. Maybe that was because vampire blood was strangely intoxicating, maybe because pain made him feel more alive. Paul gazed up at the shifting colored lights that played on the ceiling, and folded his arms behind his head. "How come we can never go back to your place, Sophie?"

She rolled over on her side and gazed at him, her icy blue eyes glowing catlike in the dark. "What's wrong with this place? Aren't you having fun?"

"I just wonder if you're keeping secrets from me."

"Everybody has secrets." Sophie laughed deep in her throat. "Are you going to tell your sister what we do together?"

Paul wondered if Sophie could read his mind. He felt himself grow hot with embarrassment. "I don't think she'd understand."

Sophie traced his nose with her finger. "That can be fixed. Make her into one of us. I hear you two are twins. We three could have a lot of fun together."

Paul drew away. "I couldn't do that. She doesn't want it."

"I didn't want it either," Sophie whispered. "Did you? Of course you didn't. Are you telling me she's better than we are?"

"Shut up, Sophie," Paul snapped. "And keep your lying mouth off my twin."

A tear trickled from Sophie's eye. The light reflected from the ceiling made her face blue, with a blue tear.

Paul wiped the tear away with his thumb. "I'm sorry," he said gruffly. "You just don't understand about Ari and me. When we were little, we even spoke our own secret language. She'd do anything for me—anything. I couldn't make her do what she doesn't want to do. She's the only person in the world I can always count on."

Sophie smiled. "But you're not going to tell her about the girl you killed tonight, are you?" Her voice turned mocking. "She wouldn't *understand*."

Paul was silent.

CHAPTER FOURTEEN

AT SCHOOL THE NEXT DAY, JESSIE SAT UNMOVING IN the commons room. Scratched on the paint beside the fireplace was a single word—HELP. He felt so desperate, he almost wondered if he had scratched it there himself.

"Jessie!" Amanda spotted him and ran sobbing into his arms. "Have you heard about poor Nadia? I can hardly believe it."

"I know," Jessie murmured. "She was so little and sweet. What kind of monster would want to hurt her?" He stiffened a little. He couldn't let on that he knew who had done it. He would never have peace until he destroyed Nadia's murderer. But how? Bullets were useless. And if he told anybody what had happened, they would only put him back in the hospital.

"It doesn't make any sense," cried Amanda. Her face was pink and shiny from crying. "I've kept going over and over it all night in my mind, and it doesn't make any sense!"

"How did you find out what happened?" asked Jessie.

"Nadia's dad called us. Nadia had told her parents she was coming over to my house to spend the night." Amanda looked puzzled. "She never showed up, though. I didn't know why she told them she was coming to my house—she hadn't mentioned it to me. It's so strange! The police found her by the canal. What could she have been doing there at that time of night? She was usually so careful! I keep thinking it's a mistake and she'll come walking in the door any minute." Amanda blew her nose. "How can she be dead?"

"We don't know the whole story yet." Jessie gulped. "I think she was up to something, Amanda. I talked to her yesterday, and I had the feeling she was hiding something from me. I think she planned to try to get to the bottom of Susannah's murder." Jessie watched Amanda closely to see how she was taking what he said.

"She tried to track down Susannah's murderer," Amanda repeated, wide-eyed, "and then she died the same way Susannah died!"

"That's what I think," said Jessie.

Amanda fell into a leather chair. "It's like a horrible nightmare," she said. "First Susannah, and now Nadia!"

"I know," said Jessie. "Her dad called me this morning with the news. At first, I guess I was in

147

shock. My parents didn't want me to come to school." Jessie did not mention that his parents had placed a panicked call to his psychiatrist. He figured the less that was said about his recent hospitalization, the better. He had spent over an hour that morning trying to persuade his parents that he was sane—and that was bad enough. They had asked him a lot of questions about when he'd last seen Nadia. But when it came right down to it, neither of them could believe that he had murdered her.

Jessie went on cautiously. "My parents wanted to make me stay home, but I told them it wasn't going to do me any good to lie in bed staring at the four walls."

Amanda squeezed his hand. "No, this is a time that we need each other. If I had to stay at home alone, I think I'd go crazy."

There was a long silence.

"What's strange, Jessie, is that somehow Susannah got the blood drained out of her, and now it's happened to Nadia."

"What do the police say?" Jessie smoothed his hair back uneasily. "I'm not even clear about exactly what happened. Nobody's explained anything to me."

Amanda looked embarrassed. "They're probably afraid of upsetting you. You know . . ." She shrugged.

"I'm not crazy," Jessie insisted. "Do I sound crazy?"

"I don't think you're crazy." Amanda hesitated.

"What happened is that the police got an anonymous phone call saying that a girl's body was on a bench near the C and O Canal."

"Can't they trace those calls?" Jessie put in a bit anxiously.

Amanda nodded. "They did. But it came from a pay phone, so that didn't tell them anything. And whoever made the call was whispering so they couldn't tell anything about his voice. The police don't have a clue about who it was. Nobody knows whether it was the murderer or just somebody who found her and was afraid of getting involved. The police went right over to the canal, of course. They told Nadia's parents she probably hadn't been dead more than an hour when they got there." She shivered. "What possibly could have made her go to such a deserted place at night?"

"Going after Susannah's murderer," said Jessie softly.

"She was going after the murderer," repeated Amanda. "If only she'd taken you with her!"

Jessie felt himself go cold. *"I used to be scared of vampires, but with you along, I know I'll be safe."* He could hear Nadia's voice echoing reproachfully in his mind. It was his fault she had died. On her own she never would have gone after Paul. Jessie would carry that guilt with him forever. Somehow he had to make them pay—Paul and that nest of vampires.

Suddenly Jessie spotted Paul. "Look!" he hissed.

149

Amanda lifted her tear-streaked face.

The hairs on the back of Jessie's neck rose. He hoped Paul wouldn't look their way. "Don't you see there's something funny about the way he looks?" whispered Jessie.

"He's pale," Amanda agreed. "But he's been sick. I think he has a sun allergy. Somebody told me he's always in the washroom slathering on sunblock."

Paul moved out of their line of sight then, but Jessie had gone cold all over. Seeing Nadia's murderer walking around free made him feel as if his heart had frozen.

Suddenly Amanda backed away. "Jessie, you don't still believe all that stuff about vampires, do you?"

Jessie shrugged.

"Are you trying to tell me Paul is a vampire?" she demanded. "If that's what you're hinting at, why don't you just come right out and say it?"

Jessie shook his head. "I'm only saying that Nadia thought Paul murdered Susannah and drank her blood. Call it whatever you want. That's what she thought, and now she's dead."

Amanda covered her face with her hands.

Ari stood in the hallway reading what was written on a poster board sign—"GRIEF COUNSELORS WILL BE AVAILABLE IN THE COUNSELING OFFICE FOR THE ENTIRE WEEK TO MEET INDIVIDUALLY WITH STUDENTS."

Cos came up beside her, and she turned to

him in alarm. "Cos, what's happened? Why is this sign up here?"

"Nadia was murdered last night." He was pale. "The police found her body on a bench by the C and O Canal. I feel like I'm going crazy. First Susannah, and now Nadia!"

"How . . . how did she die?" For a split second Ari allowed herself to think that Cos would say Nadia had been in a terrible car crash, but somehow she knew before he spoke that that wasn't what happened.

Cos shook his head. "I don't know exactly. Somebody told me the headmaster is calling an assembly. I guess he's trying to stop all the wild rumors."

Ari froze. "What rumors?"

Cos shrugged. "That she was killed by vampires."

"Oh, no!" gasped Ari.

Cos struggled to smile. "Don't you give out on me, Ari. I feel like I'm the last sane person left. Everywhere I turn, somebody's talking about vampires. I was over at the Activities Building a minute ago, and somebody had cornered the coach and was asking him how many pints of blood Sandy had had pumped into him that time he was in the hospital for his operation. People are going nuts." Cos stared at the sign. "I just hate it that all this dumb stuff about vampires is going on now when poor Nadia's stretched out on a morgue slab. It's awful. The last time I saw her, she was screaming at me, accusing me of spying on her. I never even had a chance to talk to her after that." He gazed at Ari helplessly. "You don't figure people are going to die, do you? It seems like you've got all the time in the world. . . ." He choked up.

"Poor Nadia," Ari whispered.

Amanda and Blake were sitting together on a stone bench in the school courtyard. The pale winter sun was small in the overcast sky and the courtyard lay in shadows cast by the classroom buildings. Amanda wiped her tears away with her sleeve.

"Look at it this way, Amanda," Blake said. "The only reason what happened to Nadia doesn't make sense is because you're ruling out the supernatural. You've got a blind spot when it comes to believing in something you can't see."

She gulped. "That's not true. I'm open-minded. It's just that I don't believe that evil spirits can kill people."

"Happens all the time in underdeveloped countries," said Blake. "Some medicine man puts a curse on somebody, and next thing you know, his victim is withering away."

"But that's different," Amanda objected. "It's psychological. It's caused by the power of suggestion. Besides, Nadia didn't wither away. She died very suddenly." Amanda wondered if she would ever feel safe again. One by one the people she knew were being picked off by some unseen killer.

"Open your eyes," said Blake. "All around us people are dying. There are murders every day, and beggars are whining at every corner. Some of them are talking to people the rest of us can't see. What makes more sense—that this is a rational world or that evil spirits really are walking the streets?"

"Those are societal problems you're talking about," said Amanda automatically, but she felt a sliver of doubt enter her soul. She thought about the dark cave where Blake's dad had met the oracle. That had seemed real enough to her. If strange things could happen in faraway countries, why not right here on Massachusetts Avenue?

Everywhere Ari went that morning, she saw that kids were pale and shaken. They gathered near classrooms in small groups, talking and crying.

Ari was grateful that she had no classes with Paul, because she knew she couldn't face him. He must have killed Nadia. What were the odds that it had been some other vampire? Zero.

Already Ari had heard people in the halls talking in hushed voices, saying that Nadia had died the same way Susannah had. The link was obvious. But how could Paul possibly have lured Nadia to the canal? She had been afraid of him!

Ari felt a dull ache inside that wouldn't go away. All her life she and Paul had stuck up for each other. She remembered that a neighborhood kid had made fun of her when she was five. She still hadn't been able to pronounce *R*'s. "Awi," she'd called herself. Paul had defended her. She remembered it vividly, Paul rolling around in the dirt with the neighbor kid, punching him in the stomach, pulling his hair.

Paul had always protected her fiercely, and she had tried to look out for him, too. When they had gotten to Aunt Gabrielle's house after their mother had died, they had been so scared they'd slept in the same bed. "Together forever," they had pledged solemnly. Thinking of it, Ari let hot tears stream down her face.

Later in the day all the students gathered in the chapel for the special assembly.

When the kids had taken their seats, the headmaster mounted the steps to the lectern, his face somber. "We gather here today to mourn one of our own," he began. "We grieve for Nadia, whose life was so brief. We grieve that she won't be able to go on with the rest of you to college, to careers, and to having a family of her own. We grieve for her family, whose terrible pain we can only guess. But on a more intimate level we grieve for ourselves. Our feeling of safety has been destroyed." He went on talking, but suddenly Ari spotted Paul and stopped listening.

Paul sat at the back of the chapel, one arm resting along the back of his pew. His dark eyes were fathomless, and Ari could not guess what he was thinking. If he had killed Nadia, how could he seem so calm?

154

Just then a pale, oddly dressed woman stepped out of the shadows. Her eyes gleamed feverishly, and her forehead was extraordinarily high, as if she had plucked out the first inch or so of her hair. Ari was riveted by her strange appearance and glanced around nervously, wondering why no one else seemed to be noticing her. The woman's odd headdress, a soft white cloth draped over a tall twin-peaked frame, moved softly as she walked toward Paul. Her face was the same dead white color as her headdress, and her long blond hair fell in thin strands to her waist. Ari blinked. A muscular man stepped into view, wearing a peculiar fur hat and a blue cape lavishly embroidered with gold threads. The bulging bones of his skull showed under his shiny white skin. Ari gulped as the strange pair moved to stand behind Paul, their skeletal hands folded over flat stomachs. They couldn't be real, Ari realized suddenly. Extreme stress had brought on another of her visions.

She looked away and did her best to fix her attention on the pulpit. The headmaster was outlining the sources of help available to St. Anselm's students at the counseling office. Unable to stop herself, Ari took another peek over her shoulder. She gasped to see that a crowd of vampires were standing behind Paul now, all of them with corpses' faces and deep-set, glowing eyes.

Among them was a tiny woman in a stiff, old-fashioned skirt. She had an absurdly small waist, plump arms, and glossy black hair done in sausage curls. Ari recognized her at once as the ghost from the house next door to Sybil's. Her full skirt shifted and moved like mist as she raised a plump hand and waved at Ari. "Hello!" she called in a flutelike voice.

The other vampires turned to look at her disapprovingly, but to Ari's relief no one in the assembly except Paul stared.

"Hello! Ari!" The short woman's strident voice drowned out the headmaster, and Ari was shocked to see Blake turn around and gape. It was all Ari could do to keep from answering just to shut the woman up. She gripped the front edge of her pew tightly and bit her lip, forcing herself to ignore the harsh voice that resounded in her ears. "Come back here with us, Ari," the woman shrieked. "Answer me, girl! What's the matter with you? Cat got your tongue?"

A commotion broke out on the other side of the chapel, and in her sudden alarm Ari swayed as though she might pass out. Had the vampires been spotted? Slowly it dawned on her that people weren't going toward the back but were milling around on the far aisle.

"What happened?" she asked, bewildered.

Melanie Russell stood up on the pew to see better. "Blake has fainted," she reported. "He's passed out cold. They're fanning him with hymn books, trying to bring him to." A teacher began walking purposefully in their direction, and Stephanie hastily got down. "He must be okay,"

156

she said. "He's getting up. Can you believe that? Passed out cold."

"Let us all sing together hymn number three hundred one," the headmaster hastily intoned. At once the organist began to play. They sang, raggedly at first, then with united strong voices. When Ari saw Blake being helped out the transept door, she lost her place in the hymnal. Had Blake fainted because he had seen the vampires? She glanced over her shoulder. The corpselike creatures stood singing. With their mouths open wide, they revealed their fangs.

After the hymn everyone began filing out of the chapel. Ari was relieved that the vampires seemed to have disappeared. Hoping to avoid Paul, she hurried out of the chapel along the east aisle. She squinted as she stepped outside into the brighter light. It was a chilly day, and the sky was gray. As she walked through the trees, twigs snapping under her feet, she was alarmed to see that Amanda and Jessie stood together by a large tree. Their heads were close together, and they were talking with quiet intensity. Ari desperately wished she could hear what they were saying.

"There's not a chance I can find out anything," Jessie said. "Ari and Paul don't trust me. They won't tell me a thing. It's different with you. You could go over to Ari's house and poke around." He hesitated. "I'm not saying you *should*, though. It might not be safe. After all, if

157

we're right, Paul is a murderer. You could get hurt."

Amanda pressed her fist to her mouth. "I've got to find out the truth," she cried. "I'm afraid I'm going crazy—you and Blake have actually got me wondering if Paul is a vampire."

Jessie was gratified. He had not expected to have an ally in Blake. "What happened to Blake just now?" he asked. "Why'd he pass out like that?"

Amanda shook her head impatiently. "I don't know. We were all packed in there pretty tight. It could have been the heat."

Jessie gazed up through the tree branches at the gray sky. Maybe he was crazy to encourage Amanda to poke around the Montclairs' house. It was too dangerous. "Look, Amanda, I'm not sure you should go into Paul's house alone. If something happens to you, I'm going to feel terrible."

"If I don't check it out, *I'm* going to feel terrible." Amanda's cheeks were flushed. "I can't let myself think about how scary it is, Jessie. I just have to go ahead and do it."

Jessie ran his finger around the inside of his collar. It seemed to have grown uncomfortably tight. He wondered if he had lost his nerve. No way would he go into that dark house. And here was Amanda volunteering to do it. It made him feel like a coward. "I wish there were some way you could call for help if you got in trouble inside the house," he said uncomfortably. "Some kind of panic button or some-thing."

"If you're worried, you can wait outside for me," said Amanda.

"But what good will it do me being out on the street if Paul is cutting your throat inside the house?"

"I can always scream," said Amanda impa-tiently. "I can't see how all the high-tech panic buttons in the world could be better than a good scream."

Jessie had the feeling that Amanda didn't know what she was up against. He had tasted real fear, and he knew the first thing it did was rob you of breath so that screaming was impos-sible. A gasp had probably been all Nadia had been able to get out before Paul tore into her throat.

Silently they walked back to the classroom building. Jessie desperately wanted to help Amanda, but he couldn't think how. Bullets and sharpened stakes had already turned out to be no use.

"When are you going to do it?" he asked when they reached the building.

"This afternoon," Amanda said, lifting her chin. "Why wait?"

So soon! Jessie was filled with panic. He hated feeling helpless. It made him remember how it had been to be a child in the grip of masked terrorists, unsure what was going on. He had promised himself he would never get in a situation like that again. But now he was in worse shape. His enemies weren't even human.

Instead of going to class Jessie went to the school library. Usually it took a research paper to make him get anywhere near the place, but today he had a special reason for going there. He went unhesitatingly to the computerized card catalogue and pressed the key for SEARCH— TOPIC. Then he typed in bold letters, VAMPIRE.

There were some things he needed to know.

CHAPTER
FIFTEEN

AFTER SCHOOL ARI WAITED FOR PAUL BY THE CAR. She watched cars full of students drive by her as the parking spaces emptied out. At last she realized Paul was not coming. Perhaps he was afraid she would ask him about Nadia.

Ari drove off, her head spinning. Where could her twin be? She was aware that he had another life she knew little about. Lots of times it seemed to her that he was out most of the night. It was a mystery to her how he kept up with his homework. She hardly knew him anymore; he was becoming a stranger. And maybe she should be glad. Everything she found out seemed to be bad.

Ari heard Carmel working in the kitchen when she got home. She was surprised to see that a letter lay on the small table at the entrance, weighed down by the black statuette of a rooster. She turned the envelope over curiously and saw that it was addressed to her in block print writing. It had a Charlottesville return address. *Rab*, she thought in dismay.

Ari took her books upstairs and changed into jeans. When she tried the door to Paul's room, she saw that it wasn't locked and that he hadn't been home. Usually the first thing he did was fling his book bag on the bed. Then he pulled off the tie required by the school's dress code and draped it over the bedpost.

In her room, Ari's eyes were drawn at once to the chess set at the foot of her bed. The pawn was standing upright! It had warned her that Nadia was going to die, and now that she was dead, the pawn's eerie life had left it. It was no more than an ordinary chess piece. Ari sat down suddenly on the bed, her heart pounding so hard she felt dizzy. Why had the spirit world reached out for and beckoned her as it had in the chapel?

Absentmindedly, she picked up Rab's letter and ripped it open. A single sheet was covered with the same block letters that were on the envelope.

Hi!

I know you think this is crazy, Ari. I think it's crazy myself, but I keep having the feeling that you're in some kind of trouble. Won't you tell me what it is? I know that sometimes it's easier to

162

talk to someone who's a little apart from things. I might be able to help— you never can tell. Do you still have my phone number? Remember, you can call me anytime. I want you to know that I'm thinking about you. Whatever happens, you can count on me.

Love,
Rab

Ari heaved a sigh. Sybil had once confided that she yearned to be a femme fatale and have all kinds of males falling for her on first sight. That only showed that Sybil hadn't tried it and had no idea how embarrassing it could be. Ari still remembered with painful vividness the time a neighbor in New Orleans had proposed marriage. He had been a thin man with a prominent Adam's apple and had helped her write a program for her computer science course at school. Then one day out of the blue he had asked her to marry him!

"But, Mr. Patterson, I'm only fifteen!" she had exclaimed.

"Call me Howard," he'd said. "Don't worry. I'll wait for you."

"But I don't love you!" she had said finally, running out of the house. She had run all the way home.

The last thing she wanted to do was to get into that situation again. She crumpled Rab's letter up.

Suddenly she heard the sound of the doorbell. "I'll get it, Carmel," she yelled. She ran downstairs and flung open the door. To her astonishment, Amanda stood before her.

"I was hoping I could get the chemistry assignment from you," Amanda said.

"Read chapter ten and review the lab notes," said Ari. She tried to close the door, but Amanda was already pushing her way inside the house.

"If I could just look over your notes . . ." Amanda said, her eyes darting around the dark hallway.

Ari shot a nervous glance over her shoulder. She was uneasily aware that Aunt Gabrielle's house looked strange. She had once joked to Sybil that it looked as if it had been decorated by the Munsters.

"I don't think my notes are that good," protested Ari. "They wouldn't be much help to you."

"What an *interesting* house." Amanda clapped her hands. "I've never been inside one of these old Georgetown houses. Do you mind if I take a look around?" Without waiting for an answer she strode down the long hallway. "Goodness, how elegant!" she cried, her eyes darting around the dining room as she stepped into it. "Do you have velvet curtains on every single window? That's kind of unusual, isn't it?"

"My aunt likes velvet," muttered Ari.

"Odd candlesticks," Amanda said, picking up

a silver candelabrum. "It isn't every day that you see antique candlesticks drilled for electric light-bulbs, is it?"

"My aunt worries about fire."

Amanda stepped into the servants' hallway. Ari was grateful that the door to the dark back staircase was closed. She had a morbid, irrational fear that it might be smeared with blood.

Carmel peeked her head out of the kitchen. Her face was moist with steam. She poured out a cheerful stream of Spanish, and to Ari's horror Amanda answered her. Beaming, Carmel came out of the kitchen, drying her hands on her apron. The two conducted a fluent, rapid-fire conversation, and Ari felt a trickle of cold sweat going down her back. Was Carmel telling Amanda about Aunt Gabrielle's strange sleeping habits?

"Hadn't we better get those lab notes for you, Amanda?" Ari interrupted.

Amanda laughed a silvery laugh. "I'm sorry. I know it's rude to speak a foreign language someone else can't understand. I just don't get much chance to practice my Spanish." She allowed Ari to lead her away.

It occurred to Ari that this unnerving visit from Amanda was coming at a peculiar time. Amanda had been Nadia's best friend. It didn't make sense for her to be worrying about getting lab notes the day after Nadia's body was discovered. "I haven't gotten down to doing my homework yet," Ari said, shooting a quick glance at

Amanda. "It's hard to feel like chemistry is important at a time like this. I was completely wiped out by the news of Nadia's death."

"Were you?" asked Amanda in an odd voice.

Ari stared. "Weren't you?"

Amanda lowered her voice. "I'll tell you something in complete confidence, Ari."

Ari gazed at her in amazement. Why would Amanda be confiding in her? Her pulse quickened with a consciousness of danger.

"I think Nadia was trying to track down Susannah's killer," Amanda whispered. "It's very possible she unknowingly put herself in a risky situation."

Ari felt the blood drain from her face.

"Do you see what I'm getting at?" Amanda went on relentlessly. "Susannah's murderer killed Nadia because Nadia was on his trail."

Ari licked her dry lips. "I heard a lot of kids saying something like that at school," she said. "But I don't really have any of the details. It seems very strange."

"Yes. It is strange." Amanda's words had heavy emphasis.

Ari's breathing quickened. It was desperately important for her to act the way an ordinary innocent person would act. She let Amanda follow her up to her room to get the chemistry notes.

Amanda glanced around the dark hallway when they got upstairs. "You'd think your aunt would want more natural light up here," she said.

"Putting in an extra bathroom blocked that front window," said Ari. "Come on. This is my aunt's bedroom up here. My room is in back."

Amanda did not move to follow her. Instead she ran a finger over the dusty feathers of the stuffed crow that stood by Aunt Gabrielle's room. "Your aunt certainly has offbeat taste," she commented, glancing at the locked bedroom door. "Smoked mirrors, stuffed birds, heavy curtains." She lowered her voice to a whisper. "Don't worry. I'll be very quiet. Carmel tells me she sleeps all day."

"She teaches night classes," said Ari sharply. "That's why. Do you want those lab notes or not?"

"I want them! I want them!" Amanda glanced curiously at the blood-red carpet as they moved down the hallway. "Which one is Paul's room?"

"Why would you want to know?" asked Ari coldly, reaching for her bedroom doorknob.

"I'm so curious about how other people live," said Amanda. "I'll bet *this* is his room." Before Ari could stop her, Amanda had flung open the door to Paul's room. She boldly stepped in.

"You'd better not go in there," cried Ari.

"Oh? Why not?"

"I'm beginning to think you didn't come over for those chemistry notes at all," Ari snapped, following her. "All you seem to want to do is nose around where you don't belong."

"Why would I want to do a thing like that?"

167

asked Amanda. Her bright eyes darted around Paul's room. Suddenly, to Ari's horror, she fell to one knee and lifted the dust ruffle of Paul's bed. Paul had carelessly left his coffin poking out from under the bed slightly, and Amanda's sharp eyes had spotted it.

Ari leaned against the connecting door and closed her eyes. It was all over. Amanda obviously knew Paul was a vampire. When she opened her eyes, she saw that Amanda had pulled the coffin out in an awkward maneuver that had wrinkled the rug under it. "It's . . . it's a coffin!" Amanda cried.

Ari noticed with detachment that Amanda's hands shook as she unlatched the coffin and pushed it open, exposing its padded satin interior.

"He's not in here," said Amanda. Her chest was heaving and she was pale.

"What would he be doing in there?" demanded Ari. "It's just something he keeps around for fun."

"For fun?" Amanda looked as if she were about to faint.

"For its shock value. You know, like boys keep snakes and tarantulas. Personally, I think it's kind of sick, but Paul's very proud of it." Ari was pleased with her impromptu explanation. She was feeling more in control now.

Amanda stood up. "Where is Paul?" Her eyes were unfocused.

Ari shrugged. "Out. He's met a girl who goes

to a different school, and he's always off with her these days."

"Oh," said Amanda.

"Do you want those chemistry notes now?"

"Sure." Amanda's voice was colorless. "That's what I came for."

Ari heard the rattle of raindrops on the window and glanced up uneasily. It had begun to rain.

CHAPTER
SIXTEEN

AROUND PAUL THE DARKNESS WAS COMPLETE. IF IT hadn't been for his glowing eyes, he couldn't have seen his hand before his face or even found his way to this underground place. He gasped, painfully pulling himself up to the rough cement shelf in the giant culvert and stretching out on it. Listening to the quiet sound of trickling water, he clutched his hands to his aching head. Was he dying? His skin was burning, and he felt oddly detached, as if he were losing his grip on the earth.

For the past few days he had had an uneasy feeling that he was somehow coming undone. His father and Aunt Gabrielle had warned him not to try to live a normal life, and now he wished he had listened to them.

He felt a slight weight on his pants leg and lifted his head to find himself staring at the red,

170

close-together eyes of a rat. Groaning, he bent his knee and rolled over. The rat scurried away with tiny squeaks. Paul was suddenly overcome with nausea. Some instinctive need for complete darkness had sent him running desperately to this dark bolt-hole. He had the feeling, though, that something was wrong down here. The sound of running water was growing louder.

Gathering his strength, he slipped off the shelf. Sure enough, the water, which had been only a slimy film when he'd crept into the culvert, was several inches deep and had begun to move like a stream. A flame of panic flared within him. *It must be raining hard outside.* He had no idea how high the water in these underground pipes could rise.

Paul held his head in his hands. The pain was blinding, but he realized he had to leave this hiding place. Even if he died from the sun, it was better than being swept out to sea with the rats.

The water rose to his ankles as he made his way out, and by the time he reached the mouth of the culvert, it was nearly to his knees. His feet were squishy in his stinking black tops, and when he stepped out into the gray street, he realized that his school tie was streaked with green slime. He stripped it off and turned his face up toward the falling rain. The cold, hard pellets felt good on his burning skin. How close was he to home? he wondered. He had left school in a panic and had found the culvert only by instinct, drawn to the darkness he so desperately needed.

Suddenly lightning lit up the street, and a huge explosion of thunder rattled the nearby shop windows. Paul could feel the thunder's vibration in his feet. He glanced up at the sky and saw more lightning leaping in an arc from cloud to cloud.

What were the odds of being struck by lightning in a storm like this? he wondered. Probably pretty good. But if he were dying anyway, what could it matter? He slipped off his shoes, left them lying in a gutter, and haltingly began walking. Each step was agony, and he gasped with pain.

At last he saw the familiar landmarks of Georgetown through the diagonally slanting rain. Traffic lights swayed in the wind, and gutters rushed with water. The headlights of cars were pale smudges in the downpour. Paul was feverishly hot. His meager strength seemed to be slowly leaking out through his fingers.

The pansies at Aunt Gabrielle's front door had been flattened by the storm, and the planter was full of water, its surface pitted by the falling rain. Paul staggered down the garden path and came in the servants' door, with the confused idea that he would track less water in the house that way.

Weakly he pushed his wet hair out of his eyes and tried to catch his breath. The world seemed to be expanding and contracting around him, changing alarmingly in size and shape as if it were a great balloon. He was blinded by odd flashes of light. He was afraid his time was running out. Groping his way past the kitchen, he opened the door to the stairs and began dragging himself like a wounded animal up the dark servants' staircase.

The stairs shifted under his feet as if he were on a pitching boat, and he almost fell headfirst. He grabbed the handrail frantically and gasped for breath. He wanted to see Ari before he lost consciousness. If he could say good-bye and tell her he was sorry, then he knew he could die in peace.

His trembling hand was on the doorknob of the top landing when he suddenly heard voices. The shock sent adrenaline surging through his veins. He recognized the timbre of Ari's voice, but it took him a minute to place the other one. It was Amanda!

"So you don't have any idea where Paul is?" Amanda was fidgeting nervously with her hands and darting uneasy glances around the hallway.

"Do you know where your brother is every minute?" asked Ari.

"My brother is five years old," said Amanda. "Of course I know where he is."

"Well, I don't keep tabs on Paul," said Ari.

The old house shook with thunder. Any minute Aunt Gabrielle might step out of her room, her violet eyes burning with an unearthly light. Ari knew that rainy days had a way of waking vampires from their coffins. All it would take would be one glance at Aunt Gabrielle to remove any doubts about whether this house was filled with vampires.

"It's pouring outside," Ari said. "Why don't I give you a ride home?"

"I brought my own car," said Amanda. She looked around the hallway as if she were vaguely puzzled.

"I hate to kick you out," said Ari desperately. "But I have to be going myself."

Amanda moved downstairs with excruciating slowness. The girl seemed almost in a trance. Her face had an odd look of intense concentration, as if she were doing math problems in her head. At last Ari opened the front door, and Amanda stepped out into the rain. The shoulders of her jacket darkened, and her dark hair became plastered to her head at once.

"See ya," said Ari. She closed the front door firmly, locked it, and leaned against it, breathing hard. Ari promised herself she wouldn't open it even if Amanda beat on it and rang the doorbell over and over again. She felt she had done a pretty good job of concealing the truth, under the circumstances. But she hadn't liked the look on Amanda's face one bit. She had to warn Paul.

When she stepped back into the upstairs hall, she stopped short. A dark sodden figure was lying prone near her bedroom door. Then she took in the black curly hair, the familiar jacket. "Paul!" she shrieked. She ran over to him and fell to her knees. She touched his cheek gingerly.

He felt cold, but she could feel his breath on her fingertips.

"Aunt Gabri!" she screamed. Her heart stopped when she realized Amanda might still be standing outside the front door and might hear her. She leapt up and ran to bang on Aunt Gabrielle's door. Thunder rumbled as if the sky were sounding a warning.

Aunt Gabrielle threw open her door. Her face was white, and her hollowed cheeks reflected the violet glow of her eyes. In her thin, white gown, with her black hair tumbling in wild darkness over her shoulders, she looked as if she had risen from the grave.

"It's Paul," Ari sobbed. "Something's wrong with him."

They ran together down the hall. Aunt Gabrielle felt Paul's cheeks with her hands. "I pleaded with him not to go out in the daytime," she cried. "Even this weak winter sun is so very dangerous. Ari, help me get him into the coffin."

The two of them lifted him with difficulty and awkwardly carried him into his room. Paul was barefoot and his black hair streamed a trail of water on the floor. "You really think we should put him in the coffin?" Ari asked faintly. Putting him in the coffin seemed ominous to her, as if they had given up on saving him. He was breathing, but his closed eyes looked sunken, and he was dead white.

"He'll be more comfortable there," Aunt Gabrielle insisted.

They lowered him into the narrow coffin and tucked his limp arms and legs into its satiny interior. Ari noticed that his hair left a green tinge on the satin, and her heart stopped. The green slime clinging to him gave her the sinking feeling that his body had already begun to decompose. Paul's cheekbones seemed to press close against his hard white flesh. She felt helpless and desperate. However angry she had been at Paul for the things he had done, she knew suddenly that she needed him to live. He was all she had, her oldest ally. How could she live without him?

Gabrielle closed the coffin and wiped her wet hands on her gown. "You had better go now, dear," she said. "I'll take care of him."

"What if—what if he doesn't make it?" cried Ari. "I should stay here to be with him."

Aunt Gabrielle shook her head. "Try not to worry. I'll do my best. But I can't help him with you in here."

Ari went to her room, tears welling in her eyes. What horrible vampire things was Aunt Gabrielle going to do to him? The blood-red carpet in the hallway was dark with a large uneven splotch where Paul had collapsed. He must have walked in the rain for miles, Ari realized. She wished she hadn't driven off from school and left him. Had he been forced to walk all the way home? Was what had happened to him somehow her fault?

* * *

Something lay lightly on Paul's eyelids. He tried to brush it away but couldn't. Someone's cold hands held his arms and wouldn't let him move. The familiar satin of his coffin brushed against his cheek as he struggled, and when his eyes flew open, he saw a flash of gold. Aunt Gabrielle's pale face floated like a vision over him, her violet eyes glowing with a strange and shifting intensity.

Paul's head ached, and suddenly he remembered. He had been trying to get to Ari's room when everything had gone black.

"Where's Ari?" he asked thickly.

"Don't worry—she's nearby. She helped me get you in here," said Aunt Gabrielle.

"I want to see her."

Aunt Gabrielle laid a cool hand on his forehead. "Do you feel like getting up, dear? You and I need to talk."

Paul struggled to a sitting position. He noticed that Aunt Gabrielle quickly folded a napkin into a little packet. He heard a faint metallic *chink* when she placed it behind her. "What's that?" he asked.

She smiled. "None of your business, you bad boy. You gave us such a scare!"

Paul pressed his hands to his aching head. "I don't know what happened. All of a sudden it felt like I was dying."

He struggled out of his coffin. His wet clothes were sticking to him. Even his underwear was plastered to his skin. "I'd better get into something dry," he said. But a fit of dizziness made him sit down on the bed suddenly.

Aunt Gabrielle pursed her lips. "You've got to promise me you won't try to go back to school," she said.

Paul hesitated. He was in no shape to argue, but he wasn't ready to give up on school. "I won't go this week anyway," he agreed. "Not until I figure out what happened to me."

"I *know* what happened. You're killing yourself by going out in the sun, Paul."

"I've been slathering sunblock on me five or six times a day," Paul protested.

"What about your eyes?" she asked.

"I could wear sunglasses," he mumbled.

"The sun creeps in your eyes and weakens you," insisted Aunt Gabrielle. "Some sun must filter through the sunblock as well. A blast of bright sun might kill you at once; this insidious leakage is killing you inch by inch."

Paul remembered his nightmarish climb up the back stairs and shuddered. "Okay, I'll quit school."

Aunt Gabrielle beamed at him. "Splendid. There are all sorts of interesting things one can do at night, you know. You could continue your education with tutors, take night classes, or you might even get a job. I expect you'll find that after a while you won't miss school a bit."

Paul heard a rapping on the connecting door. "It's Ari!"

Ari's frightened face peered at him through

178

a crack in the door. "You're better."

"Yeah." Paul looked down self-consciously at his clothes. "I'd better change."

He pulled some clothes from the dresser, went into his bathroom, blotted himself dry, and changed. A glance in the mirror showed his sunken cheeks and feverish eyes. Maybe it was just as well he wasn't going back to school. Right now it tired him out even thinking of trying to pass as human. He toweled his hair and ran a comb through his curls. The weakness in his knees made him wish he had grabbed that rat when he'd had a chance back in the culvert. If he had bitten off its head and drunk its blood, that might have given him strength.

When Paul came out, Ari and Aunt Gabrielle were talking. They looked up at him.

"Paul," Ari said, "Amanda saw your coffin."

The room whirled around, and the next thing Paul knew, Aunt Gabrielle and Ari were holding him up.

"Sit down," cried Aunt Gabrielle.

Paul collapsed onto his bed. "I heard Amanda talking when I came up the back steps," he muttered. "Why was she poking around over here?"

"She insisted on coming inside, and she nosed all over the house," said Ari. "Then she burst into your room."

"Why did you let her?" cried Paul. "Why didn't you stop her?"

"I tried!" Ari twirled a black lock around her finger nervously. "It was awful. I had to keep

179

acting like I didn't have anything to hide, so I couldn't very well tackle her and shove her outside."

"What did you say about the coffin?" Paul asked quickly.

Ari shrugged. "I told her you kept it for a kind of a joke. But I'm not sure she bought it. Turns out she speaks fluent Spanish. She talked to Carmel. She could have found out all kinds of things that way. I don't know what, because I couldn't understand a word they were saying." Ari hesitated. "I saw her talking to Jessie after that service today."

"I'm not worried about Jessie," said Paul. "His stupid bullets can't hurt me, and if Jessie starts talking about vampires again, they'll only lock him up."

"I'm not so sure," said Ari. She glanced at her aunt. "They had a special assembly at school today because of Nadia's death."

Aunt Gabrielle's white hand went to her throat. "Who is Nadia?"

Ari looked at Paul reproachfully.

He jumped up. "Okay, I admit it—but they were trailing me."

"What?" Aunt Gabrielle blinked.

"Nadia and Jessie followed me the other night when I left the house. I was on my way to meet Sophie. Next thing I know, they're behind me. Well, I couldn't lead them to Sophie, could I? So I doubled back and surprised them."

"Oh, Paul," moaned Aunt Gabrielle. "When will you learn?"

180

"It was self-defense," Paul snapped. "They pulled guns on me. Jessie unloaded a whole revolver at my chest. I'll show you the mess they made of my blue jacket if you don't believe me."

"But bullets can't hurt you, dear," wailed Aunt Gabrielle.

"They didn't know that, did they? They were trying to kill me. It was self-defense. Jessie got away."

"But this Jessie person must have seen the whole thing!" cried Aunt Gabrielle.

"He just got out of the loony bin!" said Paul. "Nobody's going to believe him. I think he knows that, too, because he hasn't told a soul. If he had, the police would have already come after me."

"He's said something to Amanda," Ari pointed out. "I saw them talking."

"He's trying to stir people up, that's all," Paul insisted. "He's not about to tell anybody what really happened."

"It's pretty clear that Amanda suspects you," said Ari. "And she's not just out of a psychiatric hospital. Face the truth for a change, Paul. This means trouble."

"Paul's dropping out of school," said Aunt Gabrielle.

Paul glanced at Ari. "I've got to," he said grudgingly. "I can't keep burning the candle at both ends, going out night and day. I guess that's why I'm in such bad shape."

"Now that Paul's dropping out of school," said Aunt Gabrielle hopefully, "maybe it will be a case of out of sight, out of mind. Those rumors will simply blow over."

CHAPTER
SEVENTEEN

A FIRE CRACKLED IN THE FIREPLACE, WARMING THE cabin. "We need to let it die down some more before we can roast the marshmallows," said Conner.

"Roasting marshmallows isn't exactly what's on our minds, is it?" asked Blake.

Jessie scanned the group of kids gathered around the fire and cracked his knuckles nervously. His feelings had been mixed when Amanda had asked him to come out to Conner's cabin. In a way he was glad, because this might be his chance to make the others see Paul for what he was. But he had to be careful not to take any chances. He was scared he might say something that would land him back in the hospital.

"I didn't know what to think when I pulled that coffin out from under Paul's bed."

Amanda's eyes widened. "I mean, that must clinch it. Paul *has* to be a vampire."

"Oh, come on!" said Sandy in disgust.

"But how can he be a vampire?" cried Conner. "There's no such thing."

Amanda shrugged. "Well, *you* explain why he has a coffin in his room."

"Maybe he's eccentric," said Conner. "I read one time that some famous actress slept in a coffin."

"Ari tried to tell me it was like that," admitted Amanda. "She said that Paul liked to have it around for the shock value—the way some boys keep tarantulas or snakes."

"So why couldn't that be true?" said Sandy. "It makes a lot more sense than . . . the other thing. That's just stupid."

"I phoned around town and priced coffins," said Amanda with a significant look. "They're really expensive."

"It's not as if Paul's folks are short of money, is it?" said Sandy. "Come on! The aunt drives a Mercedes."

"I know. But there are a lot of things that don't add up," said Amanda. "Tell them what happened to you, Jessie."

Jessie felt sweat break out on his brow. "I don't want to go first. Somebody else start."

Melanie turned to the redheaded boy beside her. "Sandy, tell us about how you ended up in the hospital."

Sandy turned pink. "Look, I don't want to go

184

talking about my operation. I'll start sounding like my grandfather. He never shuts up about his. No, thanks."

"But didn't you pass out at a cross-country meet?" insisted Melanie. "That's what I heard. You spent the night with Paul, and the next morning you passed out at the race, and they had to pump pints and pints of blood into you to save your life."

"Yeah, but there was a perfectly logical explanation for that. I forget the name for it, but the doctors explained it all to me."

"Yeah," said Jessie, "but you told me yourself that nothing showed up on the lab tests. So the doctors were only guessing about what was wrong, weren't they?"

"Tell us exactly what you remember about the night you stayed with Paul," Melanie prodded. "We're only trying to get at the truth."

"We had a nice dinner," Sandy said, "and then I spread out my sleeping bag on Paul's floor and went to sleep." He shrugged. "End of story."

"Sandy was sleeping in Paul's room," Melanie whispered.

"Big deal!" cried Sandy. "You make it sound perverted."

"No, I didn't mean that. I just mean that if Paul is a murderer, it might have been dangerous," insisted Melanie. "Tell us what happened."

Sandy looked at the fire. "To tell you the truth, I kind of had a lot of wine at dinner, and it's not all real clear in my mind. I'm not used to wine at dinner, and I guess I drank too much. We went upstairs and I went right to sleep."

"Did you hear that? He had a lot to drink that night!" Melanie looked around the circle meaningfully.

"This is stupid," said Sandy, standing up suddenly. "You guys are just trying to stir up trouble, and I don't want to get mixed up in it." He took a deep breath. "I think I'd better be going."

"Hey, don't go," cried Conner. But Jessie saw Melanie grab Conner's hand, signaling him to be quiet. He made no further protest as Sandy left. Jessie heard his car rev up, and a moment later the car drove off.

Melanie broke the silence. "Sandy's in love with Ari," she said. "So he's bound to be on her side. We shouldn't have asked him to come out here in the first place. He would only cause problems if he stayed."

Conner looked down at his hands. "Something happened to me that I've sort of wondered about." Jessie turned to look at him. "It happened a week or so ago," he went on. "I was in the bathroom at school and Paul came up to me."

"Yes?" Melanie prodded him.

"To tell you the truth, I got this creepy feeling he was going to make a pass at me. He leaned over kind of close to me, and . . . I don't know . . . things got a little fuzzy there for a while. I went blank and I felt woozy. When I got

186

outside, I thought for a minute I was going to pass out. I had to sort of back up against a wall to keep from falling. I felt light-headed and kind of sick to my stomach. I remember Paul asked if I needed any help. I was weak for days. But I never did run a fever or anything. My mom thought it was weird. She took me in to the doctor, and he said my hemoglobin count was low and asked if I was eating right. Mom's been pushing spinach at me ever since."

"His hemoglobin count was low," repeated Melanie in a low voice. "I think we know what that means. He lost *blood*."

"I was fine after a few days, though," Conner added.

"That's kind of what happened to me, too," Jessie ventured softly.

"You mean something happened while you were in the bathroom with Paul!" exclaimed Blake. Jessie could almost see him making a mental note to avoid going into the school bathroom. A few months ago he would have laughed at Blake's cowardice, but he was in no mood to laugh at him now.

"Nah, this didn't happen at school," Jessie said. "And I was alone with Paul's father when it happened. Say, have any of the rest of you met his dad?"

They all shook their heads.

"He's really a funny-looking guy." Jessie hesitated. "Actually he looks kind of like Paul. The weird thing is that he looks so young." He glanced around. "Of course, the light wasn't that good. We were in a bar on M Street."

"Was anybody else there with you?" asked Conner, looking embarrassed.

Jessie clenched his fists. Conner was obviously saying that he couldn't believe Jessie. "Cos went along with me that night," he said in a strangled voice.

"Too bad it was him," said Conner. A couple of the others rolled their eyes sympathetically. Everyone knew Cos was useless as a witness. He would never say anything against Ari's brother.

"Cos and I bought a couple of beers," Jessie said, "and all of a sudden in comes Paul and his dad. Mr. Montclair shows us a neat little pistol he had with a skull on it, done in jewels. I wanted to see how accurate it was, and he offered to take me out back in the alley and show me."

"If he's anything like Paul, I'd have been scared," said Melanie, shivering.

Jessie shrugged. "He was showing me how to work the safety catch, and suddenly things got weird. I'm kind of vague about what happened at that point. But after we got back inside, I could hardly stand up."

"That's the way it was with me!" cried Conner. "It was like my legs had turned to rubber!"

Blake looked around the room. "Do you realize that if we're right about this, both of you guys are lucky to be alive?"

Conner was pale. "Do you think Paul's dad

drank your blood, Jessie? Did anybody take your hemoglobin count afterward?"

Jessie shrugged. "Heck, no. I figured I was coming down with the flu. Stayed home from school a few days, watched a lot of reruns. The funny thing was that I knew that something I couldn't quite remember had happened. It was, like, sort of a partial amnesia."

The others looked uncomfortable. Jessie had the feeling he shouldn't have mentioned amnesia. That would get them wondering if he was crazy. It was Paul who had done this to him—taken Nadia from him and had slapped a "crazy" label on him so he had to watch every word that came out of his mouth. Anger was burning in his stomach, but he didn't dare show it. He wished he could strangle Paul—he wanted to stomp on his face until he felt the bones crunch under his shoes.

"I think we could put on some marshmallows now, if we want," said Conner, jolting Jessie out of his black thoughts.

They strung marshmallows on coat hangers. Then, gathering around the fire, they held them, wobbling, over the red coals.

"It's so strange when you think about all the missing blood." Melanie chewed on her bottom lip. "It all seems tied together. Sandy had pints pumped into him at the hospital. Then there was Conner's blood test that shows he had lost blood. What happened to Jessie sounds like more of the same."

189

"But what really hits you in the face," put in Blake, "are the murders. Missing blood again. Somebody told me that Susannah's throat was cut, but there was hardly any blood where she was found."

"What happened to all that blood?" cried Susannah excitedly. "It was the same with Nadia, wasn't it?"

Amanda's eyes brimmed with tears. "Poor Nadia," she said unsteadily. "I can't even stand to think about it."

"From what I could tell from the newspaper," Blake said, "it was the same. She bled to death, but it wasn't as if there was blood all around her body, because there wasn't. The newspaper said maybe she'd been killed somewhere else and the body was moved. But what if she wasn't?" He lowered his voice. "What if a vampire drank her blood?"

A collective shudder gripped them.

Amanda frowned. "But even if we're right, I don't see how we can ever get solid proof. I thought I had it with the coffin, but now I don't know. . . ." Her voice trailed off.

Jessie didn't notice when his marshmallow caught on fire. With a quick glance at his face, Amanda jerked it away from the flames and blew it out.

Jessie buried his face in his hands. "I saw it," he blurted out. "I saw him kill Nadia."

They all stared at him.

"How, Jessie?" cried Amanda. "Why didn't

you say something before? Why didn't you tell the police?"

Jessie gulped for air. "I thought everybody would say I was crazy. I was afraid!" He saw Conner's gaze meet Melanie's in a meaningful look. "Okay," he yelled, "tell me I'm crazy if you want. But I saw Paul kill her."

Blake started to speak, but Amanda put a hand on his knee to stop him. "What happened, Jessie? Tell us."

"Nadia and I weren't sure what he was up to, see? The plan was I was going to follow him, just trail him and see what he did. Nadia said she wanted to go along. She sort of made me take her. I wish I hadn't."

"You're the one who told the police where the body was," said Amanda. "Aren't you?"

He nodded. "I didn't know what else to do. I guess Paul knew we were following him. Nadia and I were standing by those stairs that go down to the canal path. I wanted to go down after him, and she didn't want me to. All of a sudden he says, 'Looking for me?' And we turned around and there he was!"

"He must have doubled back," said Blake.

"He came at me," cried Jessie, "and I unloaded half the revolver at his chest, but he kept coming at me and grabbed me. I guess I passed out. When I came to, I looked over at the tree and saw them together on the bench. They looked like they were making out." He gulped.

"Did she scream or anything?" whispered Melanie.

Jessie shook his head. "I don't think she could. I knew right away something was wrong. I couldn't see her face—his head was in the way—but I could tell she was slumped, and her toes were sort of pointing toward each other. She didn't look right. That's why I guess I panicked. I started firing again."

"You must have missed him," said Blake.

The others looked at each other. It was common knowledge around the school that Jessie had dead aim.

"Maybe I did," Jessie said humbly. "I don't know. But he got up and started coming toward me, and I saw there was blood smeared on his face."

"Jeez, what did you do?" gasped Blake.

Jessie felt himself go hot. "I ran away," he mumbled.

A long silence fell. Jessie couldn't bring himself to look at the other kids' faces. He had told the truth. If they locked him up, he couldn't help it.

"Blood on his face," Blake repeated numbly.

"When I came back, he was gone and Nadia was dead. I didn't know what to do. I knew nobody would believe me, so I called the police from a pay phone, and then I got out of there."

"I believe you," said Amanda. She glanced at Blake.

Blake took a deep breath. "Me, too," he said.

Conner looked desperate. "Yeah, but even if it's the truth—what can we do? You heard Jessie say there wasn't any way to kill the guy. He tried. He shot him again and again. *There's no way to kill vampires.*"

"Are you sure you hit him, Jessie?" asked Blake.

Jessie gulped. "I swear, the first few shots were at point-blank range. I could see the powder burns on his jacket."

"He could have been wearing a bulletproof vest," put in Conner.

"Right," said Amanda sarcastically. She looked around at the others. "Or he could be a vampire."

"What good does it do for us to say that?" cried Conner. "Even if it's true, all it means is that there's no way to get rid of him."

Amanda's eyes were hard. She thrust her marshmallows into the fire and watched as they caught fire. Then, as the other kids watched, holding their breath, she pulled the coat hanger out of the fire and held it up before her like a flaming torch.

"I just might have an idea," she said evenly.

CHAPTER
EIGHTEEN

PAUL LEANED AGAINST THE BAR AND STIRRED HIS Bloody Mary with a swizzle stick. "No more homework, no more books, no more teachers' dirty looks," he said gloomily.

"It doesn't matter about quitting school." Sophie let her hand rest on the back of his neck. "You need to take care of yourself, Paul. You don't look so good."

"Thanks a lot." He upended his drink and took a deep, gulping swallow. For once he was glad to get the pasteurized, stale blood they peddled at the bar on M Street. He felt too weak to get any other kind. He glanced up at the cadaverous, bald bartender who silently handed him another drink.

"I've made a big mess of things," Paul said.

The bartender flashed his fangs in a humorless smile. "No more than the rest of us, buddy."

"Joe hears everybody's troubles," Sophie said. She played with the hair at the back of Paul's neck.

"Stop it!" said Paul. "That tickles. Jeez, my life is a cliché. I'm telling my troubles to a bartender."

"Would you like me to read you a poem?" asked Sophie shyly. "It might cheer you up."

Paul struggled to smile. "Sure," he said.

She pulled a bit of tightly folded paper from her jeans pocket and smoothed it out on the counter.

"No flesh gilds your bones
And in your heart is darkness,
But broken in your eyes, a glowworm sings
To me.
Come feed on me in darkness, love,
And rock me in your cradle,
For in the dark I feel your heat, and
Day breaks
At last."

"Cool," said Paul, smiling.

Sophie wrinkled her nose. "But what do you think of the word choice? Do you think 'No flesh *decks* your bones' would be better? I mean, *decks* and *gilds* are sort of alike, because they're both a kind of decoration. 'Deck the halls' and 'gild the lily'—you know. I can't figure out which is better."

"It's perfect the way it is," said Paul. "I like

195

everything about it, and I like everything about you."

Sophie looked down self-consciously, and the strobe light at the back of the bar gave a red halo to her hair. Paul was staggered by her unearthly beauty.

"Sophie, who made you?" he asked abruptly.

"I'd rather not say." She gulped. "Don't be mean, Paul."

"Was it Dubay? Just tell me that."

She shook her head. "I'm not going to say anything, because then you'd just ask me was it this one, was it that one, and there'd be no end to it. Let's talk about something else."

He watched the reflection of the bar lights in the stale blood that filled his glass. "Isn't it true a vampire always has a special bond with the vampire that makes him?"

"I don't know." Sophie looked frightened. "I need to be going." Edging away from him, she folded her poem and tucked it in her pocket.

Paul slid off the barstool. "I'll go with you."

"I'd rather you didn't," whimpered Sophie.

"What are you hiding from me?"

"Nothing!"

"Then why won't you let me go with you?" He smiled. "Just part of the way."

"Okay, but only partway." She stood up and turned toward the door. Suddenly she blanched.

Paul saw that one of his aunt's friends, Gwendolyn, the graphic artist, had just walked in with a muscular vampire. The man looked toward him, and Paul saw an earring glitter in one nostril. It was Dubay. Paul felt rage swell in his throat, but he knew he couldn't let Sophie see how angry he was. He waited until he could control his voice before he spoke. "We can go out the back way," he said.

"Okay," she agreed, looking relieved.

They slipped through the crowd. The strobe light moving at the back of the bar was disorienting, and Paul was glad to step outside into the alley. There heavy rain had made the ground slick with puddles, but the night air felt washed clean. Paul let the door to the bar swing shut behind him, closing away its light and noise. He drank in the dark silence of the alley. "I love your blue eyes," he said, backing Sophie against the wall.

She giggled.

Paul nipped her neck playfully, but his arms on either side of her held her immobile. "Who made you, Sophie? Tell me." She squirmed. "Tell me!" he insisted. "Tell me now."

"Let go!"

He carelessly slapped her face, and her cheek glowed phosphorescent in the darkness. "Tell me. I'm not going to be able to sleep until you tell me. I want to know."

"No, you don't." Her blue eyes burned like iridescent jewels, and he shivered.

Paul pushed her down roughly. She lay on the ground, making no effort to get up. Her lovely face in profile showed hair clinging in damp wings to her cheek. Paul sank to one knee and pinned her under his body. He could feel wet tears on his face, but desperation seared him. If he had to, he would shake it out of her. "Why are you making me do this, Sophie?" he cried. "Tell me the truth, for once! You owe it to me. I want to know."

"No."

He squeezed her throat and shook her until her head rattled against the ground. He could hear her fangs clicking together. "Tell me!" he pleaded.

"Let go!" she gasped.

Paul released his grasp. He felt sick and disgusted with himself, but he did not get up.

"Richard," she spat. "Richard made me. Now are you happy?"

Paul rocked back on his heels, dizzy with shock. "Richard?" he repeated numbly. "My father?"

Sophie struggled to her feet.

Paul was ashamed to see the phosphorescent marks of his blows glowing on her neck and her cheeks. She was radiant with phosphorescence, and her luminous head seemed to float above the darkness of her shirt. She smiled bitterly. "You're a lot like him," she said.

He leaned against the wall, stunned. "Sophie, are you a spy for my father? Is that the only reason you've been going out with me?"

She didn't answer. He watched her silently as she walked away down the dark alley.

* * *

Blake and Amanda walked past a neon-lit bar on M Street. Amanda glanced in the open door and saw pale faces gleaming in the darkness. A strobe light flashed in her eyes. It occurred to her that it could have been this very bar where Jessie had met Paul's father.

"Do you know why I believe Jessie?" she asked Blake as they walked past the open door.

Blake shook his head.

"It's because he told us he ran away. He would never say that unless it was the truth."

"You must know." Blake shrugged. "You know him better than I do."

"Don't you believe him?"

Blake hesitated. "Yes. Yes, I do."

It was a comfort to Amanda to have Blake walking beside her. She could not imagine him running the way Jessie did. The hard set of his jaw, his faintly curling lips, and that broken nose made her think of Roman gladiators who killed lions with their bare hands.

"This is their neighborhood, you know," Amanda said.

Blake glanced around the crowded streets. A group of college students lurched toward them. "Here?"

"Not this street, of course. But in Georgetown," she said. They passed a restaurant that had bottles of wine displayed in its window. "Paul's house is only a few blocks from here. We could easily run into him or Ari."

"Nothing could happen to us here where the streets are full of people," said Blake, as if he were trying to reassure himself.

"Look, we don't really want anything to eat, do we?" said Amanda suddenly. "Let's go back to the car. I'll show you where their house is."

"Do you have something in mind?" he asked sharply.

She shook her head. "No. Not tonight. We'll just look. You've got to promise me we'll get out of there fast if we see one of them."

"Don't worry!" He was pale.

Blake didn't seem like the sort who would believe in the supernatural, thought Amanda. But there was something mysterious about him. As they passed the neon-lit bar again, she glanced at him and saw that his face was colorless. His eyes shifted uneasily.

"What's wrong?" she whispered.

"Nothing." He licked his lips. "I guess it's nerves."

She gave him a sharp look. "Blake, you don't know something about Paul that you're not telling me, do you?"

He laughed humorlessly. "How could I, Amanda? I barely know the guy."

A few minutes later they climbed into Blake's car. The windows frosted over with their breath. As they drove off, Blake turned on the blower, and its hum made a quiet backdrop to Amanda's voice as she gave him directions.

After a few blocks, the Montclairs' house

rose on their right. Its windows were darkened by the thick curtains, making it conspicuous among the other brightly lit houses.

"Jessie came with me before," Amanda explained, "when I went in to check things out. He waited outside for me."

"He shouldn't have let you go in there alone," said Blake.

"He couldn't very well go with me, could he?" said Amanda. "They already know Jessie's onto them. He wouldn't have gotten past the front door. It was different with me—I could pretend to be asking for homework."

"You were taking a big chance. Do you figure Ari realizes you know what's going on?" Blake let his car roll slowly past the dark house.

"I don't know. Maybe she thinks she fooled me."

Once they were safely past the house, Blake's tight grip on the steering wheel relaxed. He took a deep breath. "I don't know, Amanda. When I look at that house, it all seems awfully real." He shot a quick glance at her. "Do you know what I mean?"

"You aren't getting cold feet, are you?"

"It's just that I keep wondering if there isn't some other way."

"We've been all over that," said Amanda impatiently. "We know crosses are no help. You saw Paul sitting in the chapel where there are crosses all over the place. He didn't turn a hair. Nadia wore a gold cross around her neck! It didn't help her, did it?"

"It's just superstition, I guess." Blake wiped the windshield with the back of his hand, leaving a wet streak across his line of vision.

"Jessie tried bullets." Amanda ticked off alternatives on her fingers. "And it's not like we can sneak up on Paul when he's sleeping and drive a stake into his heart."

"Besides," said Blake, "while we were busy driving a stake into his heart, other vampires might gang up on us."

"You're right." Amanda gazed sightlessly at the street ahead. "Ari must be a vampire—it stands to reason that twins are the same—and the aunt has got to be in on it. The father sure is, and for all we know he's in the house, too." Amanda clenched her fists. "We've got to do something!"

"Yeah, but that stuff we talked about doing the other night at the cabin . . ."

Amanda looked at him sharply. "You're not trying to back out, are you?"

Blake shook his head. "I didn't say I was backing out. It's just that what we're planning is awfully risky."

"Sitting around doing nothing is risky, too. Look what happened to Susannah and Nadia."

"If we go through with it, we could get in a lot of trouble."

Amanda put her hand on his knee. "Blake, we're already in a lot of trouble. You know they're vampires, don't you?"

He nodded. "Yes. I'm sure of it."

"Then we can't sit around talking. We've got to do something!"

Blake was pale. "I guess you're right."

Ari heard Paul come in. She was alarmed at the dragging sound of his footsteps. Was he still sick? She rapped on the connecting door.

"Come in," he said.

She pushed the door open. "Is anything wrong?"

Paul looked at her helplessly for a moment, then fell facedown on the bed. The book lying on his bed bounced with his sudden weight. "Everything's wrong," he said in a muffled voice.

"It's your girlfriend, isn't it?" asked Ari, relieved that it was nothing worse. "You two have a fight or something?"

"Yeah." Paul rolled over, and Ari was startled by the bleakness in his eyes. "There's nobody in the world I can trust, Ari."

"You don't think you can trust me?"

His eyes darkened. "Yeah, but I'm in this vampire thing by myself." He sat up on the edge of the bed and cried, "It's so lonely!"

His unhappiness made Ari's heart twist. He had only asked her to become a vampire so they could be close. Was that too much for her twin to ask of her?

Paul viciously threw the book across the room. It struck the wardrobe with a dull thud and slid down. "Do you have any idea what it's like to look out on all eternity and not have one

203

damn thing to look forward to?" he cried.

"Everybody has times they feel low," said Ari. "You're just upset because you had this fight with your girlfriend. After you make up—"

"We're not going to make up," Paul interrupted her. "We're finished." Paul gazed into her eyes, and Ari felt herself go cold. "Vampires are bad, Ari," he said in a low voice. "I can't trust them. Not one of them."

"What about Aunt Gabrielle?" she protested. "You can trust her."

Paul's eyes narrowed. "I wonder."

"Paul!" cried Ari. "She saved your life!"

A light leapt behind Paul's eyes. "You're right. She did!" He jumped up and began pacing the floor. "And do you want to know how I think she did it?"

Ari shook her head. She wasn't sure she wanted to hear this.

"It was the vampire gold!"

Ari jumped involuntarily. "No, Paul," she whispered.

"I saw it!" he cried. "That's what she used. I caught a little glimpse of it when I opened my eyes. I could feel something light on my eyelids, and I'm sure that's what it was."

"Gold is heavy," said Ari automatically.

"Don't be stupid," snapped Paul. "A lot of that gold was hammered thin and isn't any heavier than paper. Aunt Gabrielle had it done up in a napkin to hide it from me. I heard it go *chink*. It was the gold, all right—and you can bet it's got

204

some kind of strange power. I was as good as dead until she laid that stuff on me."

"Paul, there's got to be some reason Aunt Gabrielle's keeping it a secret!"

"Sure! That ought to be obvious. She wants to keep it all for herself."

"We ought to stay away from it," cried Ari. "It's dangerous! I know it."

Paul slammed his fist into his palm. "If I could just figure out how to get back into that fireplace. I can do it—I'm sure I can!"

CHAPTER
NINETEEN

A SHRILL WINTER WIND WHISTLED AROUND THE stone buildings of St. Anselm's. Ari remembered when the campus had been calm and lovely. But today its normal peace had been disturbed. She sensed the change in atmosphere as soon as she stepped inside. Suspicion met her like a wave. She was conscious of furtive looks. People were talking about her. It was hard to put her finger on anything definite, but conversations died down when she approached; a couple of times she turned around suddenly to catch kids staring in her direction.

"Where's Paul?" asked Sybil, catching up with her in the hall.

Ari heaved a sigh of relief. Sybil at least was behaving normally. "He's at home. He's decided to drop out of school."

"Drop out of school?" Sybil looked shocked.

"What does your aunt think about that?"

"Aunt Gabrielle realizes that Paul has had a rough year." Ari's words sounded horribly false to her own ears, but Sybil did not seem to notice. "I guess this school has too many painful memories for him. He's not sure what he wants to do."

"I guess he could take the equivalency test," said Sybil dubiously. "Or he could try another school. I know how he feels. Sometimes I want to put the pillow over my head and hide. Amanda says Nadia's parents are afraid that with so much publicity in the paper weirdos may show up at the funeral, so they're having a private service. Nobody from school is invited. I think if we can't go to the funeral, we ought to have some sort of memorial service here at school."

"That's a good idea," said Ari faintly.

Sybil glanced at her watch and grimaced. "I'd better go. I've got to take a makeup test."

Ari was sorry to see Sybil's bright hair disappear down the hall. It seemed as if the last fragment of Ari's peace of mind went with her.

Life at school should have been more normal without Paul around. But today it was as if everything had somehow become infected by some vague evil. *"Bad . . . can't trust them . . . any of them."* Paul's words whispered in the back of her mind like the nagging wind.

It was obvious that the sun would not shine today. The yellow lights inside the buildings were only feeble flickers in the gloom.

"Hi, Ari. Where's Paul?"

Ari spun around. Blake and Amanda stood ten or fifteen feet away from her, directly under the hall light.

"Paul's not here." Ari gasped. "He may transfer to another school," she went on mechanically. "Too many painful memories around here."

"Yeah," said Blake with an odd emphasis. "I guess so."

The wind slapped a loose branch against a window, and Ari jumped.

Blake and Amanda walked away, their heads bent toward each other. They had kept at a distance, almost as if they were afraid of her, Ari thought. She found herself straining to hear what they were saying, but it was no use. She soon lost sight of them in the shadowy hall.

Ari turned and hurried through the building, passing scattered groups of kids. She looked around frantically for Cos but didn't see him. The groups in the hallway seemed to draw closer to one another when she approached, as if to exclude her.

The thumbtacked papers of a bulletin board were lifted by the breeze as she hurried by. She sped past dark windows and the doors of empty classrooms.

Then, just as she had almost reached her calculus classroom, she was brought up short by the sight of Jessie slumped against a locker. His fair hair shone in the dim light. When he saw her, he straightened abruptly.

Ari lifted her chin defiantly. "Hi!" she said.

Jessie's blue eyes fastened on her. "What time do you go to bed?" he asked.

Ari wanted to make a flip answer, but she found herself unable to speak. Why was everyone acting so strange?

"Maybe you don't sleep at all." Jessie's eyes were fixed on her. "Is that the way it is with you and Paul?"

Ari turned abruptly and fled into the nearby classroom. Her calculus teacher, shuffling papers at his desk, looked up at her in surprise.

Now that she was safely inside the door, it seemed as if all the strength had bled out of her. She fell into her desk, exhausted. Outside, paper and dry leaves whirled together in small eddies. The moaning wind rattled the classroom windows.

"Is anything wrong, Ari?" asked Mr. Martin.

"I have a headache," said Ari. "It's pretty bad. I may have to go home." She realized she couldn't face an entire day at school, but how could she force herself to go back past those whispering groups in the hall? And if she waited, it only meant she would have to face them in the classroom.

Mr. Martin perched on the corner of his desk and regarded her nearsightedly as he polished his glasses. "We're seeing a lot of stress-related absences lately," he said. "Headaches, stomachaches—I guess it's not too surprising."

Ari pressed her fingertips to her temples. "The past few weeks have been terrible," she whispered.

Mr. Martin put his glasses back on and peered at her with concern. "If the headache's really bad, Ari, you'd better not drive. Call home for someone to come get you, or take a taxi."

"I'll do that," she said. Hoisting her book bag over one shoulder, she lurched out of the classroom.

There was no longer any sign of Jessie in the hall outside. She darted out the first door she came to. As soon as she stepped outside, the wind whipped her hair in her face. Whirling sand turned to grit in her mouth, and her eyes blurred with tears.

"Ari!" Cos called.

Blindly she stumbled toward him. When they met, she buried her face against his shoulder and burst into tears.

Cos led her to a corner where the buildings formed a pocket of protection against the wind. "Hey." He tilted her chin upward and smiled at her. "What's the matter?"

She smiled at him tearfully. "Oh, Cos, everybody's acting so strange. They keep looking at me."

"I know," he said, shrugging ruefully. "Me, too. Maybe it's the stupid vampire rumor. We won't buy into it, so all of a sudden we're outcasts. I used to think people liked me, but lately

I feel like I'm carrying some fatal communicable disease—only nobody's bothered to tell me." He glanced up at the sky. "This weather's not helping. Talk about getting on a person's nerves!" He grinned at her suddenly. "Let's go inside and watch the others act weird, huh?"

Ari shook her head. "I'm going home. I've got a headache."

"A headache?" He frowned. "It's not a migraine, is it?"

Ari shook her head. "I just need to lie down in a dark room somewhere and get away from all this stuff at school." She forced a smile. "Mr. Martin says it's stress. There's a lot of it going around."

Cos planted a kiss on the top of her head. "Take care of yourself, okay? I'll call you."

As she walked away, she glanced over her shoulder and caught him looking after her anxiously. She waved and tried to smile. But as she walked to her car, she felt terrible. Her headache was fake, but she couldn't tell Cos that. She couldn't turn to him or ask him for help, because what she was going through was beyond his understanding. He was as comforting as a warm and sunny day. The problem was that he had nothing whatsoever to do with her life.

Ari drove her car downtown and pulled up near the Reflecting Pool. Paul had murdered Susannah here—this was where the trouble had begun. A gust of wind rocked her car. She could hear flags clanking noisily against flagpoles.

A Chevrolet pulled out of a parking place just ahead of her, and impulsively she pulled into the space. She turned up her jacket collar and got out. As she bent into the wind, grit peppered her bare legs. Her eyes squinted against the flying sand as she struggled to the Air and Space Museum nearby.

She was startled by the sudden silence when she stepped inside the museum. Her skin felt numb from the pounding wind, but in the quiet her fists unclenched. She felt confused and unclear, and she wandered as if in a dream, gazing at the outmoded aircraft that hung suspended from wires in midair. She caught a glimpse of her reflection in a glass display case and quickly closed her mouth. The white outline of her pointy incisors startled her. Aunt Gabrielle had once referred to them as "baby fangs." It terrified Ari to think she bore some sign of her vampire heritage.

She glanced at a clock and felt the familiar pull of routine. *I'd better go home and do my homework,* she thought. But first she glanced at a space rocket on display. Mannequins muffled in astronaut's gear looked trapped, with no room to sit down or run. Like her. She was hurtling into the black unknown with no freedom to escape. Suddenly Ari felt short of breath. She was convinced that a catastrophe was hanging over her.

Amanda looked around at her classmates as they passed under a streetlamp. Their faces were as expressionless as masks. "What if we're wrong?" she whispered.

Blake squeezed her hand. "We're not wrong." He carried a heavy stick topped with rags that were wrapped tightly with wire. As Amanda glanced behind her, she saw a number of other such makeshift torches grasped in pale hands. The smell of kerosene made her feel sick.

"Now remember, you're supposed to ring the doorbell," Jessie said. "We'd better not show ourselves. We don't want to scare them off. But don't worry. We'll be right behind you."

"She knows that," said Blake shortly.

"I'm going to be all right," said Amanda, as much to reassure herself as the others. "I know they're afraid of fire, because they didn't even have real candles on the table. If they make one threatening move, I'll fire up my torch. They won't dare touch me then."

"I just hope you get a chance to light it," muttered Blake.

Amanda climbed the steps and jabbed at the doorbell. Her torch was tucked under one arm. She could not resist casting a glance at the kids hiding in the shadows nearby. Unexpectedly Blake ran up the steps and stood at her side, his jaw set. After a second's hesitation, Jessie followed, motioning for the others to stay hidden. Amanda was momentarily thrown off-balance by this change of plans. Then a sudden light blinded her as the door flew open. A painfully thin woman stood facing them. Her flesh was startlingly pale, and her high cheekbones were so sharply defined, they seemed to cast shadows. Black hair flowed wildly onto her thin shoulders, and her lavender eyes glowed with an eerie and glimmering light.

Amanda's misgivings dissolved, replaced by hot panic. There was no doubt that the woman before her was a vampire. "Is Ari home?" she asked, her voice unsteady.

"I'd like to see Paul, too, if he's around," added Blake.

The woman's eyes shifted. "I'm not sure whether they're home," she said. "I'll have to check and see."

Ari wasn't certain what had awakened her, but she lifted her head from her desk in alarm. She realized that she must have fallen asleep over her homework. Now the very stillness gave her the feeling that something was wrong. It was as if the world were holding its breath.

Suddenly Paul banged on the door, making her jump. Ari flung the door open.

"Can you hear that?" Paul demanded. "Somebody's downstairs talking to Aunt Gabri. I don't like it."

"I'll go see what's going on," said Ari.

"Not without me you don't."

The twins galloped down the stairs. Ari's heart leapt to her throat when she recognized the voices coming from the open front door—Amanda! Blake!

"Paul, go back to your room," she cried. "And lock your door. I'll handle this."

"Is somebody looking for me, Aunt Gabrielle?" Paul yelled.

"Paul," Aunt Gabrielle commanded, her voice sounding strained. "Go to your room."

"No! We want to see you, Paul," yelled Jessie. "Come on down."

"I'm afraid I have to ask you to leave," Aunt Gabrielle said. "This is my house, and while you are in it, you will behave in a civilized fashion."

Ari peered over the railing at the landing. She could see that Aunt Gabrielle was blocking the foot of the stairs with her extended arms.

"Paul has not been well," Aunt Gabrielle said, her voice trembling, "and he isn't up to having visitors."

"I think we know exactly what's wrong with him," said Jessie in a nasty voice. "Come on down, Montclair!"

Ari tugged on Paul's shirt. "Don't go down there," she whispered.

"I'm not afraid," Paul said, plunging down the steps.

Ari was close behind him and she saw them—Jessie's fair head showed just beyond Aunt Gabrielle's thin, outstretched arms. She recognized Amanda, and behind her was Blake, his brutal face looming over the others' heads.

"There he is!" snarled Blake. "Get him!"

Ari smelled the torches before she saw them—the pungent scent of kerosene.

"You will go no further!" Aunt Gabrielle's voice was quavery, but her outstretched hands were pressed firmly against the doorjamb on either side, blocking the way.

"Go back, Paul," Ari cried. "They've got torches."

Paul hesitated, and Ari saw Jessie lunge forward. A bloodcurdling scream split the night. Ari watched in mute terror as Aunt Gabrielle turned to flame. The glowing fire outlined the black of her figure, leaping from her arms, her legs, her head, like a strange shifting garment. The sudden sharp smell brought Ari to her senses, and she half-dragged Paul up the stairs with her.

The twins stumbled into the hall and slammed the door behind them. Ari glanced around desperately. "They're setting the stairs on fire. The house is going to go up like tinder. We'd better get out fast."

"Aunt Gabrielle!" cried Paul. "They've killed her, Ari!"

Ari felt a lump in her throat, but she knew they had no time to grieve. "Run!" she shrieked. "They may not know about the back stairs. It's our only chance to escape."

Paul grabbed her hand. His flesh was cold, and she could feel his bones. "I'm not running away unless you come with me."

Ari glanced over her shoulder. Smoke was streaming in thin flumes around the edges of the door. Suddenly the wood door split with a

terrifying crack, and she saw fire behind it.
Panicked, she ran with Paul down the hall.

Paul hesitated at the door to the back stairs.
"Maybe I'd better get some things."

"Are you insane?" gasped Ari. "Didn't you
see what happened to Aunt Gabrielle?"

She pushed him into the dark stairwell and
followed after him. The smell of burning filled
the darkness, and Ari felt a dizzying jolt of
alarm. A gong sounded, and Paul glanced over
his shoulder at Ari, his eyes glowing catlike in
the darkness. "They must have reached the back
of the house, Ari. That was the gong at the end
of the hall. That means if we go down this way,
we could walk right into them."

"We've got to risk it." She squeezed past him.
"I'll go first. If they're down there, I'll yell, and
you can try going back. Maybe you can make it
out the bedroom window."

"What about you?"

"If I can't make it," said Ari in a low voice,
"I'll turn around and go out the window too."
But the window was too high to jump safely to
the stones of the patio. They both knew that.

The door at the foot of the stairs felt cool to
Ari's touch, so she judged it was safe to open it.
But when she did, a wave of billowing smoke
rushed in the open doorway and enveloped
them. Ari held her breath so as not to breathe it
in. She could hear the roar and crackle of flames
but could not make out the light of the fire.
She grabbed Paul's hand and pulled him into

217

the narrow hallway after her. Her eyes streamed with tears; the smoke was so thick, she couldn't see the door to Aunt Gabrielle's study, even though it was only a few steps from the stairs' bottom. She held her breath as she groped for the doorknob. At last she found it. She fell into the study, yanking Paul in with her.

They closed the door behind them at once, but Ari could see that smoke was leaking into the room. Her throat tickled and the study was hazy. The colors in the room were dull, and the light from the lamp on Aunt Gabrielle's desk looked dim, its beams shifting in the drifting smoke.

Ari threw open the French doors and gasped for breath as she stepped outside. Glancing over her shoulder at Paul, she was alarmed to see that he was making no move to follow her. His eyes were wild, and she had the sudden fear he might rush back to the fire.

"Come on! We can make it out through the garden," Ari urged.

"The garden's a trap," Paul said. "Look at it! It's closed on all sides except for the two paths, and they'd take us right out front."

Ari doubled over coughing.

"Are you okay?" Paul ran to her side.

She could hear the roar of the fire. "I'm fine," she gasped. "How about you?"

He nodded.

Ari could see now that the house's windows were bright with light that came from within.

218

Air whooshed noisily in the fire's heat, and she heard a loud crack, as if a beam had given way. The old wood of the house had gone up quickly, aided by kerosene. An outside wall could easily collapse on them. Ari heard a siren wail in the distance.

She ran to the garden gate. From there she could hear angry shouting coming from the front. She shot Paul an alarmed look. "I think there are more of them out front than we thought."

"We can't take that path," he said. "If the windows blow out, we'll be pinned between the house and the garage like rats." Paul leapt up on the bricked flower bed and peered around the boundary of the garden, his eyes burning in the darkness.

Bits of ash floated aimlessly in the air. Suddenly Ari saw a dark figure at the back of the garden. His cape was swept out balloon-style by the holocaust of fire. Ari's flesh crawled. She could see that blood was streaming down the buildings. It lay in pools at her feet.

"No!" Ari cried. She squeezed her eyes closed and covered her ears. "It can't be happening. It's not real."

Suddenly she felt Paul's arms around her. Ari turned to meet his gaze and felt her heartbeat becoming more steady. She looked down at her feet. There was no blood now. But the figure was still there.

"Paul," she said. "Look!"

Richard Montclair stepped across the petunias and stormed across the bricked pavement of the terrace, coming toward them. "Where's Gabrielle?" he shouted.

Paul and Ari looked at each other and couldn't speak.

Paul's father grabbed him by the shoulders and shook him hard. "Where is she?"

"She's dead," gasped Paul. "Some kids stormed the house and set fire to her."

Richard gazed at the house, his face turned red by the light of the fire. "Are you sure?"

"We saw it," said Paul.

Richard doubled over and fell to the pavement. "Gabri!" he cried.

As if in answer to his cry, an explosion sounded, and broken glass fell with a tinkling sound to Ari's feet. She felt a burning sensation and wiped her hand across her face, then stared in amazement at the blood on her hand. Quickly she wiped her palms on her jeans, afraid of the effect the sight of blood might have on Paul and her father.

"We've got to get out of here," Paul said. "If the back wall of the house falls, we're goners."

Their father's gloved hands were trembling. "We can go up the fire escape. I know a place. . . ." His voice trailed off. He looked at them, but he seemed dazed, and Ari was not sure he saw them.

"You two go ahead," said Ari, turning to conceal her bleeding face. "I'll go to Sybil's."

"You can't!" cried Paul. "The mob might look

220

for you there. Come with us, Ari. Be one of us."
He grabbed her shoulder and pulled her
around. "What's happened to your face?" he
asked in a different voice.

Ari backed away from him. "Good-bye, Paul,"
she said quickly. "Good luck. Don't worry about
me." She clumsily wiped the blood from her
forehead. The look on Paul's face frightened her.
His dark hair was backlit by the burning house.
He must have felt its heat at his back, but he
looked ecstatic. "Don't come any nearer!" she
warned him. "Don't touch me."

She turned and stumbled away through the
bushes. The crackling of the fire sounded close
enough to swallow her up. Grabbing hold of a
branch of a tree at the back of the garden, she
drew herself up. She jumped over the fence into
the adjoining garden and caught herself on her
knees and hands. She looked around. If she
could find her way out of this garden, where the
house fronted another street, she would come
out a safe distance away from the mob and the
fire engines that were blocking her own street.

Ari felt her way along the board fence, ignoring the holly bushes that tore at her clothes.
Peering out from the prickly bushes, she finally
spotted a garden gate that looked very much like
the one at Aunt Gabrielle's house. She glanced
back at the old mansion. A strange dawn seemed
to be breaking in the garden. The trees and the
sky were tinted orange.

She pushed open the unfamiliar garden gate

and slipped into its path. She felt safer there, sandwiched closely between the two buildings in the narrow pathway. No one could see her. The shouting and noise of the fire were faint. She touched her hair and pulled away a hand greasy with black ash. Her face was still bleeding. Where could she go in this condition?

Sybil's house was only a couple of blocks away, but Ari knew she couldn't risk going there. The mob that had already tried to kill her might look for her at Sybil's.

She hadn't realized until that moment how she had depended on her aunt. Shelter, food, money, schooling—Aunt Gabrielle had provided them all. Now Aunt Gabrielle was dead! Ari shivered. In spite of everything, Aunt Gabrielle *had* loved them. With her gone, Ari was lost and alone. If she went with her father and Paul, she knew she would have to become a vampire. But who else could she turn to!

Ari fished her wallet out of her hip pocket and counted her money. She was seized by a painful fit of coughing. Maybe she would have to go live with her father, after all, she thought. She couldn't afford to do anything else. Then she spotted the edge of her driver's license and remembered that Rab had written his phone number on it.

Rab! She gazed at the numbers, written in black marker. Rab's words sounded in her ears—*"Remember you can call me anytime—whatever happens, you can count on me."*

222

Ari shivered as she limped down the street. The air was icy cold. She supposed she had been too panicky before to notice. Keeping to the shadows when she could, she walked for what seemed like a long time, until at last she saw a brightly lit gas station with a pay phone at the edge of its parking lot. What would she do if Rab was not at home? Her chest was constricted in fear as she dropped in a quarter and dialed Rab's number. The phone rang and rang again. Three, four, five, six, seven, eight. Her courage shriveled. It was far too cold to spend the night outside.

"Hullo?" said Rab suddenly.

"Rab, it's Ari. I'm in trouble." She gulped. "Very bad trouble. I don't have a car. Can you come get me?"

"Sure. Where are you?"

Glancing at the corner, she gave him the cross streets. "I'm at a pay phone outside a filling station," she explained.

"Why don't you go to Sybil's and wait for me. It's going to take me quite a while to get there."

"I can't." Her throat closed off suddenly.

"You can't go to Sybil's?"

"No. Look, Rab, I need help," she said plaintively.

"I'm coming," he said. "Stay where you are."

CHAPTER
TWENTY

AT THE BACK OF THE STATION'S PARKING LOT, ARI found a car with an unlocked door. One of its tires was off, and it didn't look as if it was going anywhere. She hid inside. She must have fallen asleep, because suddenly she was jolted awake by the sound of someone calling her name.

"Ar-ee!" Rab, heavily wrapped up against the cold, was standing by the phone, shouting for her.

Ari slid out of the car, aching all over and feeling vaguely sick. Immediately, she doubled over coughing. When she stood up, she realized she must have hurt her ankle when she'd landed in the other garden.

"Ari!" Rab gaped at her. "What happened to you?"

"It's a long story." She gasped between racking coughs. "Where's your car?"

Frowning, he led her to it. "You're limping!"

he cried, putting an arm around her. "Here, put your weight on me."

"I'm getting ashes all over your seats," she mumbled as she climbed into the car.

"Don't worry about that," he said. "Just tell me what happened." He slid in behind the wheel and shot her a questioning look.

"The house burned down." Ari's voice was harsh, and she had the sensation that it belonged to someone else. She couldn't be sitting in this warm car next to Rab and saying this. "It wasn't an accident. Some kids came after Paul and set the house on fire, because they thought he murdered Susannah and Nadia."

"Did he?" asked Rab bluntly.

Ari nodded. What did it matter now? That part of her life was over. "Anyway, these kids came storming into the house and torched it. Aunt Gabrielle is dead."

"Dead?"

"Yes," said Ari. She wasn't precisely sure whether dead was the right word for describing the end of a vampire, but it would have to do.

"I think I'd better drive you to the police station." Rab's voice had turned coolly rational. "I know you must be in shock, but there are reports and things you have to fill out, and the sooner they're taken care of, the better. Do you think you can identify any of her attackers?"

"No," said Ari. "And I can't go to the police, either."

He blinked. "Can you tell me why?"

225

She shook her head.

"Oh." He shot a quick glance at her. "Where is Paul?"

"Safe, I think." She swallowed. "He's with our father."

"But you didn't want to go with him." Rab's high-arched eyebrows rose another notch.

"No," said Ari. This was going to be harder than she had thought. But she couldn't go back to N Street, and she couldn't go back to school, so she would have to cope as best she could. "I want to stay with you," she said awkwardly. She felt her face flaming with embarrassment. "If that's all right, I mean. I can't think of anyplace else I can go. If I could just stay with you until I work something else out, it would be a big help."

"That's fine," he said. "I'd like that. Stay as long as you like."

They drove for a while in silence. Ari had the sensation she was watching herself from a distance. There was hardly any traffic on the Beltway at this hour, and she could hear the monotonous hum of the car heater. Her hands were still icy cold from shock.

"There is a problem." She gulped. "I don't feel romantic about you at all. I mean, I like you, Rab, as a person. But I'm just not attracted to you." She regarded him anxiously. In Ari's experience, boys seldom responded positively to the suggestion "let's be friends." But Rab surprised her. A slow smile spread over his face.

"That's okay," he said. His lips twitched. "It

226

would be messy if you were attracted to me. Seeing as how I'm your brother."

Ari stared at him a moment, unable to take in what he was saying. "Is that supposed to be a joke?"

He shook his head. He exited off the Beltway and headed toward Charlottesville. "I'm your half-brother," he said.

"You're serious, aren't you?"

"Never more serious in my life," he agreed. "We have the same unsatisfactory father."

Ari stared out at the white line on the highway. It had a hypnotic effect on her. How could Rab be her brother? she wondered desperately. She barely knew him. She couldn't take in everything that had happened. Aunt Gabrielle dead! The house in flames! Paul had vanished—and Rab was suddenly her brother. It was surreal, impossible, laughable. Yet it was happening to her.

Rab continued matter-of-factly. "You remember that my mother went with Richard for years in high school. It seems they kept seeing each other on weekends during college. I think that he had just left town when my mother realized she was pregnant. Pretty fast she decided we'd both be better off if Richard dropped out of our lives."

"So she married Sybil's dad," said Ari numbly.

"Maybe she'd had enough of Richard's glitz, glamour, and selfishness," Rab suggested. "She settled for reliable and boring."

Pieces of the puzzle clicked into place in Ari's head. She realized now why Rab had been anxious to meet her and Paul, and why he had

227

been so appalled to realize he had almost run down his own father with his car. Some things that had once seemed odd now made sense. She noticed with a strange sense of detachment that her hands were trembling. One thing she was sure of: Rab had no idea what kind of family he was stepping into. She took a quick breath. "Exactly how much did your mother tell you?"

Rab grimaced. "As little as possible. Also, you'll notice, she kept me out of sight. Boarding schools, summer camp, and then more boarding schools. It was like being an orphan."

Ari gazed at Rab's profile, so reminiscent of Paul's. It was odd how similar features could in one man be handsome and with only slight changes turn homely in another. No wonder she had missed the resemblance.

She looked away. "I expect she was only trying to protect you," she said in a stifled voice.

"Oh, I'm sure she was." Rab shrugged. "But it's kind of hard for a kid to accept that his mother doesn't want to have him around. It's left me bitter and scarred, the whole bit." He smiled.

"How can you joke?" cried Ari.

"I'm not joking. Didn't you notice?"

The dark road ahead flamed up and Ari saw Aunt Gabrielle, a stick figure wreathed in fire. The fire and the burning stick figure danced along the swiftly moving pavement like the phantom she knew it must be. Ari closed her eyes to shut out the haunting images. "So she never explained to you that she was only trying

228

to protect you from your real dad?" She glanced at Rab, wishing that he would smile again. Suddenly she wanted to know if his incisors were pointed.

"I didn't even know who my real dad was until I was in prep school. But I wasn't exactly surprised when Mom and I had a big talk when I was fifteen. Until then I had had the fantasy that maybe I was adopted. My theory was that my parents thought they couldn't have kids, so they got me. But then when Sybil came along, they decided they didn't want me anymore. It seemed to make sense—I sure didn't look like my parents. But it turned out the truth was more complicated." He glanced at her. "You want to tell me now why you can't go to the police? Is it because Paul killed those girls? You don't have to tell them that part, you know."

Ari was silent, conscious only of dull pain. *Paul, my lost brother,* she thought miserably. *Where are you? I'll never know now. Paul—Paul!* Her twin's name was like the fragment of a sad song that she couldn't get out of her head.

Rab sighed. "I think I may know why you can't go to the cops," he said at last. "A while ago my mother got drunk and said a lot of wild things about Richard that didn't make much sense at the time. I think she had had a bad scare when she ran into him on the street, because she was completely flipping out. I didn't know quite what to make of it, because I never had seen her in that state before. But lately I've been thinking maybe she had to get drunk before she could work herself up to tell me the truth."

"What did she tell you?" Ari blinked at him.

"That Richard's a vampire. That he murders people and drinks their blood."

Ari felt something tight inside her go slack suddenly. It was all over for her—the loving, the lies, the fear. From now on she was no longer part of a pair. She was alone. Tears stung her eyes, and she had to remind herself that the truth, however ugly, was easier than endless lies. It had to be.

"It's true, isn't it?" asked Rab.

She nodded.

"And your aunt—is that why you couldn't call the police? Was she a vampire too, like Richard?"

Ari nodded.

"Paul, too?" Rab asked, glancing at her. "Is that why you never wanted to let me meet him, why you've been looking half-crazed?"

With tears streaming down her face, Ari nodded. "That's why I couldn't go with him." She looked down at her blood-smeared hands. "I'm afraid of him."

Rab swore under his breath.

"Paul will be all right with our dad." Ari forced herself to speak steadily. "I have to believe that's true, because I can never see him again, Rab. I've got to start over somehow."

"You'll be okay in Charlottesville," said Rab.

"Nobody's going to look for you there."

Ari set her jaw. Life without Paul—it was so hard to imagine. But somehow she had to go on. "I'll get a job," she said in a quavering voice.

Rab shook his head. "Not necessary. I have plenty of money for both of us. Besides, your aunt must have been loaded. Somewhere there must be a stock portfolio or something. I'll put my dad onto finding out about it." He grinned. "My other dad, that is."

Ari saw that Rab's incisors were pointed. She gripped the armrest tightly. "Rab, didn't you tell me that you have visions?"

He shrugged. "Yeah, I do—sometimes."

Ari fell silent. It seemed as if the blackness she had left behind was reaching out for her again. Rab had the same dark heritage she did. That was why she could tell him things that Cos could never understand.

Rab nudged her with his sharp elbow. "Hey, cheer up. Lots of people have visions. Haven't you ever seen those signs in run-down neighborhoods that say, MADAME BLATOVSKY, CERTIFIED PSYCHIC. I saw an ad on the tube the other day for a psychic with a nine hundred number. She took credit cards."

Ari took a deep shuddering breath. "I guess you're right. It's okay to be a little bit psychic." How could he joke? she wondered. It was hard for her to imagine that she would ever laugh again. She gazed out the window. She had to keep telling herself that she was safe. That no one even knew where she was. She murmured, "Maybe the vampire gold did have a curse laid on it, but I don't have to worry about it anymore, because it's gone up in smoke."

"Vampire gold?" asked Rab, looking serious. "I hope your aunt didn't sock all her assets in gold. That would be a bad investment."

Ari gulped. "I don't think this was an investment. It was something else." Rab didn't have to know everything that had gone on in Aunt Gabrielle's house, she decided. It was better if he didn't. Safer. She wished she hadn't even mentioned the gold. "Anyway, it doesn't matter now. Everything burned up in the house."

"Well, cheer up, then," suggested Rab. "The way I see it, it could be happily-ever-after for you from here on out."

Ari spoke steadily, determination sounding in her voice. "I'm going to live an absolutely normal life. I won't even let Paul know where I am." She took a deep breath. "From now on, the curse of the vampire gold is finished."

EPILOGUE

THE NIGHT WAS COLD AND CLEAR, AND THE BURNED timbers of the house stood out in silhouette against the huge moon. A silver Mercedes had been backed up over the curb and was parked close to the mansion's shattered facade. It was very late, and all the houses were dark. The streetlamps, too, were dark, their glass covers broken. Only the cold light of the moon fell on the house.

Paul got out of the Mercedes and touched the brick of the house's west wall. It was still warm. The fireplace was intact. Gingerly, he climbed up through the broken facade into the soggy and charred ruins of what had once been an elegant living room. The couch was a broken, black skeleton, soaked by the firefighters' hoses. Carrying a black cloth bag slung over one arm, Paul picked his way carefully through the sodden ashes. It was dangerous, because he had to make sure each board was solid before he dared to put his weight on it. Parts of the flooring had turned to carbon, and there were nasty gaps through which he could glimpse the darkness of the basement. He could already see that the marble surface of the fireplace was blackened and cracked. His heart pounding wildly, he reached out to it and touched the unrecognizable ball of marble that had been a sculpted face. When he tried to turn it, it fell out of its cracked marble socket. The pale marble vampire face that was the other side of the device grinned up at him in the moonlight.

He closed his eyes, sick with disappointment. But a second later he was groping desperately at the right side of the fireplace. It moved! The mechanism was damaged, but he had the strength to pry it open with his hands. Bits of the shattered fireplace fell with a soft sound to the sooty floor, but Paul scarcely noticed. A quick glance had shown him that drawers behind the brick were untouched by fire or smoke.

He glanced around furtively. Fortunately, no one could see what he was doing. The part of the facade that was still standing shielded him from the street. He began pulling drawers open and shoving the contents into his bag. It took more than one trip to empty the drawers of the treasure, and Paul was breathless with excitement. The half-closed trunk of the Mercedes had a faint glow from the reflected brightness of the gold.

At last he went back and emptied the last drawer. Only a few pieces remained, and he did not bother to stuff them into his bag. A jeweled cup caught his attention. He tucked a couple of additional chalices under one arm, not noticing that one jeweled cup had slipped from his grasp and lay in the ashes. He alone now had the vampire gold! He could not resist raising the goblet to the moon in a mock toast. Silhouetted against the moon, its metal was strangely dark, a cup fit for poison. He held it up over his head and watched the moonlight dance on its jewels. His chest swelled in elation. "You and me, gold," he whispered. "To us!"

VAMPIRE TWINS 3

BLOODCHOICE

look out for the return of the
Vampire Twins in *Blood Reunion*

Lions Tracks

The Outsiders by S. E. Hinton
£2.99

This is the chillingly realistic story of the Socs and the Greasers, rival teenage gangs, whose hatred for each other leads to the mindless violence of gang warfare.

Rumble Fish by S. E. Hinton
£2.99

Rusty-James has a reputation for toughness: he runs his own gang, and attends school only when he has nothing better to do. But his blind ambition to be just like his glamourous older brother, the Motor-cycle Boy, leads to an explosive and tragic climax.

That was Then, This is Now
by S. E. Hinton
£2.99

Caught in the violent and frustrating atmosphere of an American city slum, Mark and Bryon, who had always been like brothers, now find they are drifting apart. And then one day Bryon discovers the awful truth about Mark...

Taming the Star Runner by S. E. Hinton
£2.75

Travis's life in the country with his uncle after the bright lights of New York is pretty dull, but the choice is that or reform school. The only thing to liven it up is the girl with the horse called the Star Runner – and he's never thought much of girls.

After the First Death by Robert Cormier
£3.50

A busload of young children is hijacked by terrorists whose motive is to render useless one of the major secret service units. The general heading the unit is forced to employ his sixteen-year-old son Ben as a go-between, exposing him to appalling danger.

Eight Plus One by Robert Cormier
£3.50

These nine stories probe the feelings and reactions of people in life's most trying situations: a first love, leaving for college, a boy's discovery that his father is all too human. The stories are warm, touching and intensely personal.

Fade by Robert Cormier
£3.99

Paul inherits a strange gift: the power to become invisible. At first he thinks this is a thrilling trick, but when he finds out more, he gets scared. Is the fade a gift or a curse?

Tex by S. E. Hinton
£2.99

Life is fine for Tex until he comes home one day to find his horse has been sold to pay the mounting bills. From then on things get uglier – his father seems unconcerned about the trouble Tex is in at school, and his brother is determined to force matters to a head. For Tex, the truths revealed are devastating.

Lions Tracks

The Bumblebee Flies Anyway
by Robert Cormier
£3.50

Barney has volunteered for treatment in an experimental hospital. Then he comes across the Bumblebee – a glowing red MG, shiny and apparently perfect – and gradually evolves a crazy, daring plan to fulfil his companion's one remaining dream.

The Chocolate War by Robert Cormier
£2.99

Enthusiasm is weak in the school's annual fund-raising sale of chocolates, so Brother Leon, the organiser, turns to the Vigils, a secret society among the pupils, for help. They choose a new boy as their victim: the surest way to win the Chocolate War.

Beyond the Chocolate War
by Robert Cormier
£3.50

Although months have passed since the Chocolate War, the school still festers with the memory of it. The Vigils are more powerful than ever, but the cruelty of their leader, Archie, has made him many enemies, and now they are seeking their revenge.

Order Form

To order direct from the publishers, just make a list of the titles you want and fill in the form below:

Name ....

Address ....

....

....

Send to: Dept 6, HarperCollins Publishers Ltd, Westerhill Road, Bishopbriggs, Glasgow G64 2QT.

Please enclose a cheque or postal order to the value of the cover price, plus:

UK & BFPO: Add £1.00 for the first book, and 25p per copy for each addition book ordered.

Overseas and Eire: Add £2.95 service charge. Books will be sent by surface mail but quotes for airmail despatch will be given on request.

A 24-hour telephone ordering service is avail-able to Visa and Access card holders: 041-772 2281